NO JUSTICE, NO PEACE

Episode 1: Black Justice Series

ADE DOSUNMU

After centuries of injustice, oppression and racism,
the world's tyrants finally get to face off against the
son of a Black Panther

No Justice, No Peace

ISBN 978-1-7357416-5-9

Invocation

We repeat the words of the Thrice-Great Thoth:
"Wise words, although written by my decaying hand, remain imperishable through time; Imbued with the medicine of immortality by the All-Master.
Be unseen and undiscovered by all those who will come and go, wandering the wastelands of life.
Be hidden, until an older heaven births human beings who are worthy of your wisdom."

__The Hermetica (The Lost Wisdom of the Pharaohs)
By: Timothy Freke & Peter Gandy
Tarcher Cornerstone Editions

Applied History and Anthropology

The Greek, Roman, British, Belgian, Dutch, Spanish, Portuguese, German, French, Italian and American sins have included slavery, colonization, predatory economic exploitation, systemic racism, social injustice and police brutality.

Remember this well: Blacks are an ancient group. You all came from Blacks. Blacks do not think in terms of quarterly profit-and-loss statements. Blacks think in centuries, millennia and eons. Thus, the Blacks' one billion years of payback begins. Now.

__Ade Dosunmu

Applied Ophthalmology

Develop your X-ray vision! Once you train your eyes to strip everyone of all accoutrements and appurtenances of power, title, fame or wealth, all that you will behold is the shivering soul of a naked ape.

__Ade Dosunmu

Applied Asymmetric Warfare

1) Never turn the other cheek, except to rotate and deliver a solid back-fist to the enemy's temple.
2) Never go eye for eye, for you will lose as soon as they take out your second eye. Better to cut off their head as soon as they remove your first eye, and bend down to remove only one eye from their bodiless head in the sand. Then, you have assured that the 'Eye-for-eye' rule is obeyed.
3) Love your enemies' widows.
4) If the enemy is unjust, and is too powerful to conquer, become a suicide bomber.
5) Omo t'oni iya hun onisun, ohun na ko ni f'oju kon orun!

__Ade Dosunmu

Holy Scripture

Ha-ba le-horgekha, hashkem le-horgo.
If anyone comes to kill you, arise and kill him first.
__Talmud, Sanhedrin Tracts, Portion 72 a-b

Preface: First Matters

(A Choice of Wraths)

Dramatis Personae:

Still Small Voice (SSV)

Me, Just a Regular Old Nobody (JaRON)

SSV (In the middle of the night): You, there!

JaRON (In deep sleep): Who? Me?

SSV: Yes, you! Wake up!

JaRON (Drowsily): I'm awake.

SSV: No, you are not. You need to be fully awake! Now!

JaRON: Okay, okay! My goodness, it's 2AM for God's sake! Who are you, anyway?

SSV: Never mind who I am. Just wake up. And listen up!

JaRON: Alright, fine! I'm all ears.

SSV: You have to go give America a message.

JaRON: Who? Me?

SSV: Yes, you!

JaRON: What message?

SSV: A final warning.

JaRON: A final warning?! What's that supposed to mean?

SSV: America has a final chance to make a U-turn now before it crashes.

JaRON: U-turn? Crash? What in God's name are you talking about?

SSV: For over 400 years, America has been doing evil deeds inside and outside its borders. It ends now; either because you end it, or we end you. All of you.

JaRON: Oh, God! I'm losing my mind! Why me?

SSV: Quit feeling sorry for yourself. Someone had to be chosen to deliver the message. We chose you. Deal with it.

JaRON: But I am not a good messenger. I garble up messages.

SSV: In that case, too bad for you, and too bad for America.

JaRON: Wait! Hold on! Please wait! I'm not a public speaker. I am not a writer. Nobody knows me. I'm not even on social media. Why would anybody listen to me, much less believe me?

SSV: That is their problem, not yours.

JaRON: Please, sir, is there any way I can help you find someone else to deliver your message, please?

SSV: Quit wasting time. America needs you!

JaRON: Oh, no…not me! There are so many others to choose from. I can name some perfect candidates for you…

SSV: Stop, Jeremiah!

JaRON: Jeremiah? I'm not Jeremiah. See, I knew all along that you had the wrong person. My name is not Jeremiah. It is JaRON. It means 'Just a Regular Old Nobody!' See even my parents knew I would never amount to much, that I would never do anything important, and that I would never be chosen to carry any important message or anything like…

SSV: Stop yakking, please. Jeremiah is merely a biblical reference. Jeremiah was another person just like you who tried to avoid a similar mission thousands of years ago. We know your name…we know all of your names, including the ones you yourself are not even aware of. We call you Jeremiah merely because you are behaving just like him right now. Man up! Or, better yet, God up! Nothing you have ever done in your whole life is as important as delivering this message.

JaRON: Sir, I'm very happy just as I am. I don't like doing important things. I am very allergic to important matters…they tend to make me break out in hives!

SSV: Enough! This is no longer about you! This is about 300 million Americans; men, women and children...including those yet to be born! Their futures depend on you. So, listen up!

JaRON: Yes, sir! Is it okay if I take notes?

SSV: Feel free to take notes. Tell America that it has come to the end of the road. Tell your people that we have given you 400 years to grow up and do right. Tell them the blood of victims of social injustice, racism and oppression cries out to us every minute, every day for over 400 years.

Tell America to cease and desist its evil ways. Tell America to turn around right now. Tell America that we have run out of patience, and that therefore it has run out of time.

JaRON: You keep saying we, we...Who are these we?

SSV: That information is above and beyond your pay-grade. Please focus; this is critically important.

JaRON: I hear you.

SSV: Tell America that if we witness just one more case of police brutality, racism or oppression, we will unleash wave, after wave, after unrelenting wave of suicide-bombers right here inside the heart of America. Blood will run everyday down your busiest streets. The suicide-bombing will take place continually and sporadically in places high and low: your business offices, your airports, your sports arenas, your trains, your hospitals, your schools, your courts, your police stations, your military bases, your banks, your capitol, your White House, your churches, your restaurants, your malls...We will send your own oppressed people to blow up all your places of gathering. We will utterly decimate your economy. Your infrastructure will be in complete ruins.

And all of that will just be the beginning; we have in place unstoppable plans to bury your country next to Persia, Greece and Rome. We will make your country the new Third World. And within the next 40 years, your people will be begging for their daily bread from the likes of China, Nigeria, Israel, India and the United Arab Emirates.

JaRON: Sir, nobody will believe me.

SSV: That is not your problem. They will ignore you at their own peril. America is not your world's first superpower. It will not be the last. Egypt, Byzantium, Mali, Great Britain are among the dusty relics of pulverized arrogance. We can crush America in a day. But we are giving you 40 years. Starting now! That is the message. Deliver it! Any questions?

JaRON: Yes, sir. I am afraid the American authorities will destroy my life if I open my mouth to say these things in public…or even in private. What if I refuse to deliver your message?

SSV: Either you deliver the message, and you face the wrath of the Americans; or you do not deliver the message, and you face our wrath. You have a choice of wraths to face. Take your chances!

JaRON: By when am I required to deliver the message…Sir?

SSV: By this time…last year.

JaRON: Last year?? Oh my God!

SSV: God yourself up, man! Do not be afraid. You now have an opportunity to save the lives and livelihoods of over 300 million Americans. You have the opportunity now to use your unused life to save others. Your life has no higher purpose than this: Use it…Or lose it! You can try to save your own life. Or you can try to save 300 million American lives. One or the other. You cannot choose both. You get to save one useless life. Or you get to save 300 million lives. Choose well. Goodnight!

JaRON: My   God,   my   God!   Why   hast   Thou   forsaken   me?!

Contents

Today

All systems were "Go!"

The greatest inauguration in the history of American presidency was set to begin in just a few minutes.

The Assassin, too, was ready. He felt he had been born ready for this moment.

All his life, he had watched the great American pendulum swing further and further to the left. It was time to jolt that pendulum right back to the right, where it belonged. And all he needed to make the pendulum swing his way was this special weapon he had picked up from The Old Man.

The Iron Fan. That's what The Old Man had called it. He had designed and custom-printed the weapon. A masterpiece of a weapon forged in a furnace of love's labor.

The Iron Fan rifle was one of a kind, designed to kill two birds with one stone -- so to speak, and to create unspeakable havoc in the process. The Old Man always taught that there was one and only one perfect weapon for each job. The Iron Fan could not have been more perfect for this occasion.

For the first time in American history, a pair of Co-Presidents – both women – were to share presidential powers, and run the country like a joint account.

Over my dead body, thought The Assassin. He was set to kill the two 'birds' with one shot.

The Assassin had holed out and lived inside a fake HVAC Unit since the elections in November. Patience. Grit. And his Thermoskin Chameleon full-body suit had kept him alive through the bone-cracking cold nights of Washington D.C. winters. Those, plus a 90-day supply of NASA-designed Nutripills. Better than any military ration MREs. Meals Ready to Eat. MREs were glorified bricks designed to shock and awe any normal bowel into submission. But these new-fangled Nutripills? Total space-age nutrition in a bottle! They allowed an astronaut -- or a sniper -- to stay in place for months without having any need to go. And whenever regular nutrition was resumed, the user's kidneys and bowels simply rebooted like a new-born baby.

Apart from regulating body heat, the Thermoskin body-suit also did double-duty as an Isotonic Resistance Exercise Suit. So, The Assassin could stay in place for months at a time, and still get some serious work-out time. And no sweat, literally, thanks to the Thermoskins' nano-thermoregulators

The Assassin had spent most of his adult life doing wet work for governments and corporations all over the world including a couple of jobs on space-colonies. Most of his ops were solo. Plausible deniability came with the territory. And naturally, they were mostly for Uncle Sam or for one of Sam's many global shadows.

To prep for this particular mission, The Assassin had commandeered the HVAC and phone systems of the Washington Monument with a simple SCADA hack. So, when the monument's HVAC system had suddenly "broken down" in the middle of the November winter, it had been The Assassin's disposable phone that had received the call for repair help.

Old tradecraft: start a fire inside the fortress; be the first firefighter on the scene. Enter the fortress; put out the fake fire and plant a time-bomb. Old school. Always worked

The Assassin had walked into the Washington Monument to repair the 'broken' HVAC system.

He had wheeled his Roadie case into the elevator all the way up to the pyramidion where the HVAC system was located.

Because of the 'broken' HVAC, there had been no visitors, and the grounds security had been perfectly happy to let him go do his thing 'up there'.

Starting at 9AM, 'his thing' had taken The Assassin 15 hours to complete. While pretending to mess around with knobs, buttons and switches on the HVAC instrument panel, what the Assassin had really been doing was building an AI simulacrum – an identical twin of himself.

By 2AM, he had completed the identical-twin build, and had remained holed up inside a newly custom printed nano-house he just 3D-printed inside the pyramidion.

At 0215, , The Assassin's AI twin walked past a couple of shivering security guards, pushing a clanky Roadie case ahead of him.

"Let there be heat!" The AI had said, aiming for humor. The guards had scowled. Too cold for jokes. There had been a great din and hum. And pipes and vents of the Washington Monument had roared back to life as The Assassin himself settled in nicely inside his newly constructed hiding place inside the pyramidion.

He had built a perfectly camouflaged opening in the wall of the pyramidion facing the future inauguration platform in front of the Capitol building.

He had lived on Nutripills in near-perfect silence in his hiding place for well over two months. But he had refused to be fazed by the waiting period. The mission, as far as he was concerned, was what he had waited and prepared for his whole life. And in any case, he had already established a personal record of holing up in cramped quarters for six whole months during a particularly sensitive wet-job on a space colony.

Now his two months of living and waiting for The Iron Fan to roar was about to come to a glorious end.

Four of the 12 barrels of The Iron Fan were designed to provide kill shots of two to four targets at the same time. The other eight barrels were designed to launch grenades in eight cardinal directions.

Every projectile was high velocity – all twelve powered by a single squeeze of the trigger. And the barrels were made to be angulated as needed. That was the genius of this particular weapon.

The Assassin always marveled at The Old Man's ability to predict the future, and having predicted them, would always proceed to create the perfect weapon system designed to foil the very gods themselves.

The Iron Fan, it seemed, had been created for the precise purpose of assassinating these two Co-Presidents – *these abominations*, as far as The Assassin was concerned. And The Iron Fan had also been designed to cause total pandemonium by launching grenades into the crowd, thus giving The Assassin time and chaos enough to scram before the inevitable subsequent lockdown and knee-jerk search reaction began.

The Old Man had always taught that 'real history' was always written by those who were warrior enough to place the perfect finger on the perfect trigger in the perfect place at the perfect time. And to The Old Man, that perfect trigger-finger combination of ordinary mortals more than equaled the so-called great finger of God.

And speaking of ordinary mortals, The Old Man appeared to be fast approaching the end of his own mortality. In truth, The Old Man was older than The Assassin by no more than a decade, at most. But in the military profession, a decade was the equivalent of two generations, depending on how much action the senior soldier had seen. So, everyone had taken to calling the old man The Old Man.

Too bad The Old Man was Black, The assassin thought. That was his only flaw, as far as The Assassin was concerned.

The last time The Assassin had gone to see The Old Man, it had been at a nursing home in Dam Neck, Virginia.

Kind of funny how life played out, The Assassin mused. He himself had been a plank-owning member of the cadre of the clandestine institute known simply as HELL. The Assassin had been one of the people The Old Man had invited to join him in developing what had since become known as the world's toughest military training program. He reflected on how The Old Man who had ruled a brood of vipers, all of whom had been to a man the very best of warriors on Earth, trained under deadly conditions from age three to age 21, now that same old warrior-commandant had become a drooling old bag of black skin and bones rattling beneath a glorified rag of a blanket at the old people's home.

The Assassin remembered how The Old Man had faced down multiple international human-rights organizations who had charged the institute for abusing minors, for training three-year-olds how to survive in hostile terrain. While facing the charges, The Old Man had changed the minimum age of admission to two! Realizing that they were dealing with a monomaniacal psychopath, and having the sudden need to start looking over their own shoulders, the human-rights activists had all slowly slinked back into the warm little wombs of their own mothers, and basically left The Old Man and his infamous HELL the hell alone.

Once asked by a dying student, what the hell HELL stood for, The Old Man had responded softly, cradling the student's broken body, "Heaven and Earth's Last Legion."

Crazy damn life! Now, the know-nothing doctors had said that The Old Man had either suffered a pin-stroke or was suffering from Alzheimer's disease. Or both!

The Assassin refused to believe all that stupid medical mumbo jumbo.

No matter what the white coats wanted to believe, The Assassin had detected a spark of life dancing like a firefly inside The Old Man's eyes as the two of them had sat and talked in the Zen garden of the nursing home.

The Assassin had informed The Old Man of his plan to carry out the greatest assassination of all time. At that precise moment, it had appeared as if the fire dancing previously only in his eyes had warmed the whole shriveled body and spirit of The Old Man back to life.

Animated, The Old Man had asked three simple questions, and given just one piece of advice. But the piece of advice had bothered The Assassin until he had finally laid it to rest by choosing to believe that the doctors might be right; maybe The Old Man was indeed suffering from a pin-stroke or Alzheimer's…or some combination thereof. *Whatever*!

The Assassin figured he now had ten more minutes before the inauguration ceremonies began in earnest. Before he, The Assassin of unparalleled skill, changed the course of history forever. He chose the time to calm and quiet his mind into what the samurais of ancient Japan referred to as mushin.

Still the last conversation he had had with the Old Man inside the Zen garden kept popping unbidden into his mind.

Rather than fight it, he went with the flow and replayed the conversation in his head.

Old warrior habits never die; they just molt into new forms. The whole conversation took no more than three minutes. Volumes were spoken, more with silence than with words. It was all very informally formal. Their conversation represented the best of military Special Forces informal formality.

The Assassin: "Sir, permission to carry out an op state-side."

The Old Man: "Where?" (The Old Man had taught all of them never to ask "Who?")

The Assassin: "D.C."

At that, it seemed that The Old Man had stirred to life

The Old Man: "When?"

The Assassin: "January 20th"

At that point there had been no doubt The Old Man had shown as much excitement as he was psychologically capable of displaying.

More silence.

Then, The Old Man had finally asked: "Weapon?"

The Assassin: "The Iron Fan. Sir!"

There was history with The Iron Fan.

When The Old Man had presented The Assassin with The Iron Fan, he had specifically forbidden his pupil to use the weapon unless he first obtained permission. He had also told the Assassin to reserve the weapon for his opus magnum – his greatest job.

With that, the two of them had reached an unstated understanding that whatever job The Assassin used The Iron Fan for should be his final op – a job that should be worthy of this most supreme of modern weapons.

Prior to that conversation, The Old Man had always concluded every pre-op briefing with one final statement, a bit of superfluous, but somewhat fatherly advice nonetheless: "Watch your six!" That had always been The Old Man's signal that time for talking was over; it was then time to go out and take souls, as needed.

But on that day, which now seemed so long ago, in that Zen garden at the nursing home in Dam Neck, Virginia, The Old Man's final words to him had been "Watch its six!"

Not "watch your six!" as he had always ordered, but "watch its six!"

That, from a man who never made any mistakes – a man whose whole life, words and deed had been like an infinite series of flawless plans and executions ordered seemingly into existence by flawless pronouncements – like God himself. The Old Man who, as far as The Assassin knew, had been the only man that even the denizens of shadow governments of every powerful nation referred to as "Sir".

"Watch its six!" The Assassin shook his head, totally cleared his mind, steeled his will and locked in on the scene now playing out on the inauguration podium in front of him! At least, he thought, by viewing through the stereoscope on The Iron Fan, the podium was literally set right in front of him. All that was now necessary, The Assassin felt, was for him to simply relax, reach out, and touch someone…with his own finger which he now considered to be much stronger than the great finger of God.

Both Co-Presidents were getting ready to raise their right hands in the middle of the swearing-in. And right behind each Co-President was her husband. And the two husbands were also coming into office as Co-Vice-Presidents in the next twelve seconds.

Over my dead body, thought The Assassin sitting with legs splayed wide behind the tripod that supported The Iron Fan. *Double, triple, no quadruple abomination. But, no problem, thanks to him and The Iron Fan, these abominations were about to be blown off the pages of American history.*

Ten seconds to go.

On zero, The Assassin would change the course of American history. He calmly placed his God-finger on the trigger of The Iron Fan. His breathing now perfectly centered on deep auto-pilot, sniper-mode, he counted silently.

Ten…

One Thousand.

Nine…

One thousand.

Eight..

One thousand.

Seven…

One thousand.

Six…

One thousand.

Five…

One thousand.

Four…

One thousand.

Three…

One thousand.

Two…

One thousand.

One…

One thousand.

Zero!

He   squeezed   the   trigger.

50 Years Ago

Bobby Lee Wallace discovered that pain had several levels of intensity beyond which all medications became powerless. He was now at a level where even the strongest opioids were no better than your average sugar pill.

To move was to invite the great-grandmother of all agony. So, in the ten or so hours since midnight when the first lightning bolt of pain had shocked him awake, Bobby Lee had learned to keep perfectly still.

The problem was that keeping still merely shifted some of his agony from the physical to the mental level.

Once he learned to keep still, his mind was utterly drowned in wave after wave of other people's pain and suffering. Somehow his mind was re-enacting all the injustices, all the hate, all the hurt and all the brutality he had dished out over his career to many victims, both on and off the record.

But rather than looking from the outside in, he now felt the full measure of his victims' suffering as if he had become an amalgamated victim, the total sum of all the innocent people he had wrongly ticketed, arrested, beaten, sodomized with his police baton...and in particular, that one, the Black man he had killed for the great crime of selling pizza slices on a street corner in New York.

The victim, Frederick Turner, had been guilty of buying pizza two or three boxes at a time, divvying up the pizza into strips and slices, and selling those wire-thin strips to other poor people, his customers, who wanted pizza but did not have enough money to purchase even a regular slice from a regular pizza joint.

And so, he, Bobby Lee Wallace, had used his power as a police officer to arrest and to kill Frederick Turner, the street vendor and his tiny little piece of the much-vaunted American Dream.

The news media had discovered that Frederick Turner had been an ex-convict with a family to feed. And having been deprived of all opportunities for gainful employment after his release from prison, the man – who had had the audacity to be Black and to be poor in America – had turned to the American promise of entrepreneurship. In prison, he had read and re-read Think and Grow Rich by Napoleon Hill. And then he had really tried to personalize the message for himself by also reading and re-reading the black version of the book: Think and Grow Rich – A Black Choice, by Dr. Dennis Kimbro.

In prison, Frederick Turner had visualized his goal very clearly. Upon his release, he would seek gainful employment and save up enough money to buy himself a used truck. He would then use the truck to turn himself into a pizza-plus-everything-else-legal delivery guy. He would carve out his pizza delivery niche in his old neighborhood where other pizza delivery guys would not dare to tread, but where he had earned some serious street creds for trying to bring down the criminals, who had ultimately framed him and got him imprisoned in the first place. He was willing to compete against Uber Eats and DoorDash on his own turf.

Once he had secured enough capital from his pizza delivery gig, he was going to parlay his funds into starting his own pizza parlor. He had even had the name picked out: Forten Pizza.

Many in his own family and among his friends thought his intended company name was a reference to the fact that he had gone to prison "for ten" years for a crime he did not commit.

But Frederick Turner had patiently informed anyone who cared to listen that the name Forten Pizza was his way of paying homage to James Forten – the black millionaire who championed civil rights and anti-slavery movement during the wee hours of American history.

Frederick Turner had chosen James Forten as his spiritual mentor and godfather-inheaven, and since the pizza industry tended to be associated with mafia-type godfathers and the like, his pizza would be a living *in memoriam* to his own self-chosen godfather. Thus: Forten Pizza.

That dream had died with Frederick Turner right on the pavement of a nameless New York street.

The dream of Forten Pizza had been strangled to death with a chokehold applied by Bobby Lee Wallace – a racist pig in police uniform.

Despite feeling enormous second-hand sufferings from all of his victims of police brutality, Bobby Lee Wallace had willed himself not to cry. Something reptilian, something monstrous within his soul would not permit him to acknowledge the humanity of his victims.

He was therefore surprised and annoyed when he felt wetness in his eyes and across the bridge of his nose as he lay motionless in his bed. His breathing was becoming labored and frothy.

He glanced at his bedside mirror and saw reflected back to him a pale black face with blood drops tracking from his right eye across the bridge of his nose to mingle with more blood oozing out of his left eye, dropping softly and spreading in ever-widening crimson stains on his white pillowcase. It was the shock of seeing his previously lily-white face now turned ashen black that finally unhinged him. He had now become a physical as well as an emotional mash-up of all his former victims.

That was the moment when Bobby Lee Wallace knew that he too had contracted the deadly Judgement Day Virus that had become a pandemic. The pandemic and its horrors were all over the news everyday. No one who had access to even an antique flat-screen TV could have missed the horrific descriptions of what the victims of the virus experienced in their final moments. Based on that knowledge, Bobby Lee Wallace became certain that he had less than an hour to live, that his lungs would soon fill up with blood, and that like all the other victims of the Judgement Day Virus, his final words would be: "I am guilty!"

It had started about five months earlier, on the Fourth of July, in America.

But within weeks, it had spread all over the world killing people in places high and low. There were all kinds of horror stories about tyrants and their minions morphing into spitting images of their former victims.

The last three words of every one of the infected tyrants had invariably been: "I am guilty!". Some irresistible verbal pressure within the dying perps' brains always made them confess their guilt out loud through the pink froth bubbling in their mouths. " I am guilty! Mea culpa! Mea culpa! Mea maxima culpa!" pronounced in all the world's languages. Because of this peculiar feature of the illness, the media had dubbed the mystery disease the Judgement Day Syndrome, and the global health authorities and experts had remained utterly stumped as to the cause, or the cure. No one had a clue.

The only thing that anyone knew for sure was that the only demographic group spared so far had been children.

The best brains in epidemiology and virology had met and dispersed, and had met again, only to disperse yet again with not a whit of insight into the cause or treatment of the Judgement Day Virus.

Everyone, including Nobel laureates in Medicine had all stretched their individual and collective minds past the snapping point searching for any clue about the Judgement Day Pandemic. Over 500,000 deaths later, they were still coming up empty handed.

Governments were panicking, markets were in free fall. People all over the world wanted to march in protest, but being afraid of contracting the illness from other protesters, people had had to content themselves with protesting online through TikTok, Facebook, Instagram, YouTube and Twitter.

"I am guilty!" Bobby Lee Wallace said, and his miserable little racist life ended without anyone or anything marking its passing. Even his fellow racists avoided him in his final moments. He died alone. Unsung.

On the night of December 19th, the only man in the world who knew the secret – and held the only key – to the Judgement Day Pandemic checked himself into a psychiatric hospital.

He had chosen to go in as a John Doe with bitcoins in place of a verifiable health insurance.

Dr. Randall Robinson, the psychiatrist, sat at his desk like an army general in command of a battlefield. A middle-aged man, possibly no older than maybe 45 tops, his eyes seemed trained to cut through the irrelevant and to penetrate straight into the heart of things. He looked like a man who listened with his eyes as well as his ears. And his face bore the calm stamp of one who had heard and seen it all.

His lips had the shape of a precision–crafted instrument, and when he parted his lips to speak, his voice seemed designed to mesmerize.

John Doe approved of what he saw and what he heard, but he reminded himself that he had not come all the way to this particular hospital in order to be mesmerized by Dr. Randall Robinson, or anyone else.

The John Henrik Clarke Hospital was located on the site of a re-purposed Benedictine monastery on St Simons Island. It was situated right next to Igbo Landing, the watery grave of rebellious slaves where the city fathers in a grand show of extraordinary smallness of stature and spirit had opted to erect the city sewage plant. The city fathers were so thoroughly American in their own view of themselves, they thought nothing of dumping daily sewage on graves of stolen Africans who had fought a desperate and ultimately suicidal battle against slavery in the land of the free and the home of the brave.

Igbo Landing in St Simons Island had always thus been one of those hidden treasures serving as a silent monument to American schizophrenia and hypocrisy.

And the John Henrik Clarke Hospital had been deliberately built on the grounds of Igbo Landing by the billionaire Silicon Valley tycoon Ms. Oluwatimilehin Elaine Brown.

Ms. Brown abhorred social amnesia. She felt that if America was permitted the luxury of forgetting its evil ways, such evil was likely to rear its inhumane head again and again.

So, she had gone out of her way to spend her Silicon Valley billions creating new companies and organizations that did good works while reminding the nation of its past evil. She owned many healthcare centers and what she called edupreneur incubators all over the country.

She started the John Henrik Clarke Hospital as a public health advocacy center, a senior center, a tier-one obstetric, surgery, internal medicine, pediatric and psychiatric hospital all combined; a place where anyone – including the indigent could receive world class treatment and services.

At the John Henrik Clarke Hospital, neither race, nor money, nor class, nor power nor any iota of influence got anyone any better care than anyone else. All were equally welcomed, and treated like royalty, regardless of their social status outside of the hospital. Some 'patients' were known to show up at the hospital just to refill their tank of humanity, knowing that regardless what complaints they bore, the staff would treat them with decency and dignity.

Less than ten years after its founding, the John Henrik Clarke Hospital had already acquired a reputation as the most transparent, most egalitarian, all-round best top-tier hospital, not only in America but in the whole world.

Ms. Brown had been known to quietly fly desperate patients from developing countries in her private jets – a couple of which had been retro-fitted to function as ambulances in the sky.

And she had done most of this work in the shadows. Not one in a thousand of her employees could positively identify her in a line-up.

In public, those who knew her at all thought her name was Timi Elaine Brown. But those who knew her from way back in the day swore her real name was Nyeri Mtume.

John Doe liked what he knew about Ms. Brown, which to his way of thinking, was not quite enough. But he figured that considering his reason for being at this hospital at this time, any deep knowledge of anyone other than Dr. Robinson would be irrelevant for his purposes.

And in any case, he thought, he himself even at this point in his career had many different identity cards and passports squirreled away inside vaults in all kinds of safe houses in almost every country all over the world. His life as a Special Ops ghost warrior had required him to exist at least as a chameleon whenever he could not be a total ghost.

Seated across from the doctor, the man called John Doe silently evaluated the psychiatrist for several minutes before reaching his conclusion: the doctor was absolutely unflappable – on the surface, at least. So, he decided to plumb the psychiatrist's depth and test the man's mettle. See how true the good doctor's north was.

"I am Dr. Randall Robinson. May I ask your name?" Dr. Robinson asked and waited.

"I have many names; but the one listed on my original birth certificate is Derrick Olorogun Stevens."

"Interesting name..." intoned the doctor.

"Why?' the patient asked, watching the doctor like a scientist studying a specimen under an electron microscope.

"I happen to know that Derrick means leader of his people. And that Olorogun is a military chieftaincy title in Nigeria, and it means warlord."

"Looks like your travels have not been a total waste, Doc. But have you considered your own name, doctor?"

"Yes. And I do what I can to bear up under its weight. Can't say I've had much success. I hope you, on the other hand, are faring better than I," said Dr. Robinson.

"It is part of the reason I came here," said the patient, who still had not told the doctor his current name. "I had a twin brother...His name was Eric Stevens."

Dr. Robinson let the patient speak.

"I found out about him only after he died in a very secretive nation – the most advanced nation in the world – located right in the heart of Africa. And it was not until my brother was killed in Africa that our mother revealed my true identity to me."

"I'm sorry for your loss," said Dr. Robinson.

"My gain is greater than my loss. I lost my brother, but I found my purpose."

"Purpose..." Dr. Robinson prompted.

"Yes! Four years ago, my mother told me everything about my brother, and about my father. Prior to that, up until age 33, all I did was follow a life track laid down for me long ago by my mother -- Quantum Weaponization/Artificial Intelligence / Systems Engineering, History, Philosophy and Special Ops warfare."

"That's a strange combination, if you don't mind my saying so," said Dr. Robinson.

"G-POV, my mom called it," said the patient.

"G-POV? What's that?"

"God's Point of View"

"Sorry, I don't quite get it," said the doctor.

"Quantums in order to be able to figure stuff out at the most granular level. Weaponry, to learn how to build or break down weapons. Systems engineering to learn how things work and how to make all things work. History to understand the true story of human beings. Philosophy to figure out how humanity is supposed to function at best versus the mess we have made of all things. And Special Ops in order to know how to live, and how to die as a man. As a warrior."

"Interesting. And now, with all that background, you are in a psychiatric hospital. Why?"

"Not just any psychiatric hospital. I'm in your psychiatric hospital."

"Thank you for the vote of confidence, but still why are you in a psychiatric hospital at all?"

"Because I need your help."

"For what?"

"I know all about you, Dr Robinson. I know exactly what you do outside of your cut-out psychiatry practice. So, I know you're the only person in the world who can stop me now."

"Stop you? From what?"

"From blowing up the world," the patient answered with a chilling finality. No inflection. No emphasis. No excitement.

Dr. Robinson stopped taking notes. He gently and neatly laid down his pen, and carefully swept the patient's chart aside as if to expand his view of this extraordinary patient.

"Alright, Mr. Stevens…"

"For now, Dr. Robinson, you may address me as Dr. Stevens or The Patient. Right now, my real identity is irrelevant given all that about to take place over the next twelve days. Nevertheless, should our rapport develop enough to warrant it, my true identity will be revealed to you in due course. Until then, think of me as The Patient. Or as Dr. Stevens."

"You are a doctor?" asked Dr. Robinson mentally casting about for a handle on this strange patient.

"Yes. By the time I was 21, I had been awarded a doctorate in each of my three disciplines -- QWAISE, History and Philosophy -- by MIT."

"QWAISE? What's that?"

"That's my core discipline: Quantum Weaponization/Artificial Intelligence / Systems Engineering."

"Remarkable. Very well, Dr. Stevens. Let's begin at the beginning. Please tell me all about you. And tell me how you came to know about my work outside of my psychiatry practice. But most of all, tell me – please – what you mean by this notion of planning to blow up the world.

"Sorry Doc, but we don't have time."

"What do you mean 'we don't have time'?"

"Twelve days."

"Twelve days?"

"Doc, you have exactly twelve days to stop me from blowing your world up into a zillion flaming nothings. Today is December 20th. The New Year will meet the Big Bang and that will be the end of planet Earth. The only human being who can stop me from carrying out my mission is you. And you'll have to give me a damn good reason not to do it. And...the next twelve days is all the time you've got to stop me, and save your world.

So, I recommend a maximum sense of urgency, doctor."

"Let me get this straight, Mr....Dr. Stevens; you're planning to blow the world up in twelve days? And only I can stop you? And you committed yourself to this psychiatric facility for the express purpose of making me stop you?"

"Yes," said The Patient softly, without a single iota of emotion – in the manner of a man reading a barcode: like it was what it was. Axiomatic. Mechanical.

For several seconds, Dr. Robinson remained very still, gazing intensely at his patient..

Then suddenly, he burst out laughing. "That's a really good one," he guffawed, slapping The Patient's chart on his desk in the manner of a man enjoying an elaborate, but ultimately silly prank..

The Patient stood up. "In 24 hours, there will be no Statue of Liberty, no White House, and no Buckingham Palace...and that's just for starters. Go ahead and log in to CNN, and try to have a good day, Dr Robinson." And with that, he walked out of the psychiatrist's office, leaving the latter wondering precisely what DSM-X diagnosis would be most fitting in this case.

Schizoaffective Disorder (Bipolar type)? Bipolar Zero, Profound Manic Episode With versus Without Psychotic Features? Megalomaniac Personality Disorder? What? Back in the days of DSM-V, Dr. Robinson mused, they would have tagged this kind of patient with Schizoaffective Disorder, Bipolar Type, and it would have stuck. But that was when the psychiatrists had it easy. These days, all doctors suffered mini-strokes just trying to choose a diagnosis without the aid of an AI-enabled diagnostic software.

Within minutes of the interview, "Have you heard?" became the highest trending hashtag on Twitter.

TV networks all over the world streamed local variations of the same message.

It started with a special announcement back on CNN. The notorious Anonymous V for Vendetta mask image had interrupted regular programming to warn the viewers that many iconic buildings and monuments in various countries all over the world would vanish within 24 hours.

A ticker-tape of target buildings crawled across the bottom of TV screens below the Anonymous Mask.

The Statue of Liberty.

The White House.

Buckingham Palace.

The burial site of Queen Elizabeth I who commissioned a ship named Jesus -- the first slave ship to carry that peculiar cargo out of West Africa.

The Palace of Brussels.

Napoleon Bonaparte Monument.

Maison Bonaparte.

The royal crypt in the Church of Our Lady of Laeken in Brussels where Leopold II's remains are stored.

Tweets and retweets crashed Twitter. Ten times.

No one knew who or why, only the when and a fraction of the what.

Secret Service Special Agents and crack police units crashed into homes all over the world. China. Russia. Iran. Romania. Ukraine. England. South Africa. France. Belgium. Germany. Libya. Turkey. Even North Korea. The usual suspects -- hackers -- were slammed against walls and floors. Script kiddies as well as hardcore hackers were cuffed, collared and hauled into black sites for interrogation.

The interrogators took all kinds of liberty, shocking and waterboarding suspects. No dice.

Within hours, the interrogations had escalated to include family members as young as three and as old as 93. Still no dice.

Databases and server farms were scanned, double- and triple-cross scanned. Dead ends all over the world. In the meantime, tick-tock…tick-tock…

Six hours after their first interview, The Patient was back in Dr. Robinson's office summoned there by the psychiatrist himself.

He sat and watched calmly as the doctor shut and locked his office door just to make sure no hospital staff barged in on what he supposed would be a long and intense conversation.

Shunning his desk and chair, Dr. Robinson took a seat on the other couch in the room facing The Patient who continued to watch the doctor with preternatural calm.

The Patient gave the man kudos for having balls enough to lock himself in an office with a man who had obviously been on everyone's wanted list in the past six hours.

"We need to talk," said Dr. Robinson

"I'm all ears," said The Patient, shrugging.

"What the hell is going on?" Dr. Robinson asked, breaking all manner of protocol with his choice of expletives.

"What the hell do you think is going on doctor?" The Patient shot back. Coolly. Calmly. Red ice for blood.

"You hacked CNN," Dr. Robinson said, trying to regain a modicum of professional neutrality.

"And?" asked The Patient nonchalantly.

"So, you're admitting that it was you who hacked CNN?"

"Admitting it?" asked The Patient incredulously. "No, I'm not admitting it, I'm proclaiming it. I already pretty much told you I was going to do it just before I left your office."

"But why?" asked Dr. Robinson.

"Why? Feel free to call it a teaser, a prelude, an appetizer. Call it whatever you want. That hack is a mere taste of things to come."

"Mr. Stevens, do you realize how serious this is?"

"Once again, Dr. Robinson, for now, you may call me Dr. Stevens," The Patient gently corrected the doctor.

Dr. Robinson interrupted, "Yes, yes. Dr. Stevens, do you realize how serious..."

The Patient in turn interrupted, "The real question is: do you?"

"Look, HIPAA or no HIPAA, what is to stop me from handing you over to the authorities right now?"

"Because, Dr. Robinson, right now, I am the authority."

"Sir," said the psychiatrist shaking his head slightly, "you truly are getting very seriously delusional."

"Doc," said The Patient in the manner of a teacher patiently waiting for a slow-witted student to play catch-up. "Doc, I offer you a one-in-a-billion chance to save the world, and you're about to blow it -- so to speak -- because you're not listening. You've been well trained by your medical circus masters. If you let go of your psychiatrist-circus act for a minute, and listen to me through every pore in your body and soul, you may just finally begin to grasp what's at stake here. So, do you wanna pay attention, or do you wanna play psychiatrist? Your call, Doc." The Patient placed his elbows on his thighs, steepled his fingers, leaned in, and supported his chin on the pads of his thumbs. Roles reversed, now he looked like he was the psychiatrist, and the psychiatrist was the patient.

"Okay," Said Dr. Robinson at last. "You have my attention. But first, tell me why you think you are the authority?"

"Dead man's switch," said The Patient..

"'Scuse me?"

"Kill switch," said The Patient even more cryptically. Circular explanation.

The doctor looked lost. The patient decided it was high time he gave the good doctor a break.

"Dr. Robinson, I am a dead man's switch. A kill switch."

"You mean like the type that suicide bombers hold down with their thumbs? So that if you kill them, their thumb is released and the bomb goes off?"

"Bingo! Or should I say 'boom!'"

"So, you have such a switch?"

"I do not have such a switch, doctor; I am such a switch. If you call the so-called authorities, and they rush in here to arrest or kill me – if they make any move at all that as much as stresses me out, it will take only one shake for the world to blow up after I get stressed out. Do you know what shake is, doctor?"

"A shake? Well, I'm not so sure I do, Dr. Stevens," said Dr. Robinson.

The man was learning, The Patient thought, noting the sudden use of the correct honorific.

"A shake, Dr. Robinson, is about 0.00000008 seconds. According to the humorless wit of Los Alamos scientists who worked on nuclear bombs back in the day, a shake is the amount of time it takes a lamb to shake its tail, which the nuclear scientists relate to how long it takes a nuke to go boom! Well, I have rigged things up so that the world would evaporate within one shake of me getting stressed out – or getting killed. I think you'd better prescribe me some Xanax, Doc," said The Patient dead-panning. "You don't want me getting stressed out now, do you?"

Dr. Robinson pinched himself. He looked like a man about to have a stroke.

"On second thoughts, Doc, maybe you should take the Xanax, you don't look so good, if you don't mind me saying so," The Patient offered, managing to look seriously concerned for the doctor.

Dr. Robinson took off his white coat and flung it on his desk. Then, he loosened his tie, and wiggled his neck free like a turtle.

The Patient watched wondering whether the good doctor was getting ready to implode or explode.

The game, thought The Patient, hadn't even begun yet, and the best psychiatrist in the world was already crapping his pants. No hope for humanity, he thought, trying not to shake his head to reveal his disappointment.

"The world would end in a shake," Dr. Robinson muttered, as if discussing the idea with some apparition that only he could see in the room.

The Patient thought the psychiatrist was about to lose his mind. He continued to watch to see how close to the edge of sanity the man would travel before permanently slipping away.

Dr. Robinson stared off into space for a long time as The Patient continued to watch calmly.

At last, the doctor took a shuddering breath, jack-hammered briefly, and let out an extended sigh. He seemed to gather himself as he said, "Alright, what can I do for you? How can I help put a stop to this?"

"Notwithstanding the stench from Igbo Landing, your hospital grounds are very well-appointed. They make for a pleasant walk. Come, doctor, let us take a stroll about your grounds as I tell you why I should kill the world. And you try to use your best hostage negotiation skills to stop me from carrying out my diabolical scheme!"

"How did you know about my hostage rescue works?" asked Dr. Robinson, almost bristling. "That's highly classified material. The U.S. Government…"

"Dr. Robinson, I am now the U.S. Government. For the next twelve days, I control absolutely everything, everywhere on your backwater planet."

"But how?"

"Good question, Doc. Very good question," answered The Patient, calmly, smoothly. "Come, doctor, let us take a stroll in your local Garden of Eden."

"Why?" asked Dr. Robinson.

The two men were taking what to casual onlookers appeared to be a leisurely stroll on a meandering path along the well-manicured grounds of The John Henrik Clarke Hospital. Their pace was measured as they discussed the impending end of the world. But they looked like they could have been discussing the similarities and differences between Odetta Holmes and Nina Simone, so leisurely and cadenced was their pace.

The two men were a study in contrasts. Dr. Robinson, the psychiatrist, had donned his white coat, but his necktie was still loose, which contrasted deeply with the lockjaw tension on the man's face. A short and stocky man with a leonine face capped by a great gleaming bald dome of a head.

The Patient, on the other hand, looked preternaturally relaxed in his black Nike tracksuit and matching Nike sneakers. He was tall and lithe, with a carefree but disciplined athletic stride. His face was a magnet, effortlessly commanding the attention of the onlooker. But like the face of an avenging angel, there was an element of implacable finality etched upon his rugged features. His was a face no normal person would wish to confront during the day, much less in a dark alley at night. His face had the unforgiving integrity of Ogun, the African god of iron and warfare. It was a face that neither asked for nor offered any quarters. The kind of face that always made the already puny Napoleons of the world shrivel further into their shells like salted snails.

His lips looked perfectly resolute as if genetically engineered to command and control armies in a relentless march across the Alps, lips bred and shaped to issue orders that would bring Rome to her knees to complete the unfinished symphony of Hannibal, the Carthaginian.

Oh, but the eyes! The man's eyes flamed like an acetylene torch, expressing the focused fire of his soul – a soul that appeared to be a focal point of untold generations of African grandeur and goodness cooked to perfection by millions of years of pure African sun. The patient sported eyes divine enough to make the gods bow. And those very dangerous eyes now smiled almost like a prayer of benediction as Dr. Robinson repeated his question, "Why?'

"Why?" The Patient echoed. "Because there are only three possible outcomes in any contest: win, lose, or draw."

"What contest are you talking about?" Dr. Robinson asked.

"It doesn't matter what contest. For every contestant, every contest must end in a win, a loss, or inconclusive, otherwise known as a draw. That's Game Theory 101."

"But my question is why are you planning to blow up the world?"

"Because the history of mankind is a record of the ongoing contest between good and evil. And for all of that history, evil has been the reigning champion – reigning uncontested sometimes for centuries at a time."

"So, good has been losing?"

"It's not even close," said The Patient.

"How close?" Dr. Robinson asked.

"Good: ten. Evil: ten billion!"

"Terrible odds," ventured Dr. Robinson. "Insuperable."

"No," said The Patient. "Not insuperable."

"How is that?" asked Dr. Robinson.

"Well, because the good may not win the contest," replied The Patient. "But it doesn't necessarily have to lose either. The contest could always end in a draw."

"How so?" asked Dr. Robinson again.

"By stopping the contest."

"But how do you stop the contest?" Dr. Robinson realized he was fast becoming a question-machine. But the psychiatrist in him had melded completely with his hostage negotiator alter ego. "How can one stop a game played out daily all over the planet by billions of people?"

"Blow up the stadium. Kill the arena. Game over," The Patient answered with implacable finality.

"But ten billion to ten…" Dr. Robinson began tentatively.

"Yes?"

"Who are the ten billion? And who are the ten?" Dr. Robinson asked.

The two men had been strolling the grounds so deep in conversation they had failed to notice the approach of two little girls about age nine or ten – one Black, the other white, both bald.

Cancer. Chemo.

"Would you gentlemen care for some Girl Scout cookies?" the girls chimed in perfect unison. "My best friend and I," the two pointed to each other, "we are competing against other besties to see which Best Friends Forever will sell the most Girl Scout cookies!"

Dr. Robinson looked at the girls and blinked like a motorcyclist who just dunked his bike into a swimming pool right in the middle of a highway. The incongruity of the situation flash-froze the psychiatrist's brain. For a moment, Dr. Robinson became Dr. Ice-Cubesfor-Brains.

The Patient's eyes smiled as he watched the blinking psychiatrist, and the BFFs waiting for a response.

"But where are the cookies?" Dr. Robinson finally managed to croak, his voice sounding strangled, like a priest delivering a sermon inside a sinking boat..

Again, in perfect chorus – like mental conjoined twins – the two girls chimed their response together: "We're just asking for names and phone numbers for now. Once we get to the deadline, we'll submit our list, and when they bring us our supply, then we will find you and bring you your orders. No matter what, we are the BFFs who are going to win this contest! Would you gentlemen please commit to helping us win the contest?" the girls asked breathlessly.

"When does the contest end?" Dr. Robinson asked.

"December 24th" answered the BFFs. "Just in time for Christmas!" The two girls, like most kids, had a monopoly over exclamatory speech.

Dr. Robinson looked at The Patient. The latter cocked his left eyebrow, a mischievous smile dancing more in his eyes than around his lips. The look of innocence was priceless.

Dr. Robinson looked back down at the kids. "Very well," he sighed "My friend here and I will take as many cookies as you need to sell in order to win." He finished and looked surprised at himself at what he just said.

"Yes-s-s!" the two girls shouted, pumping their fists and high-fiving each other. "Alright, let's take your names and numbers. And we promise to bring you a bunch of the best Girl Scout cookies in the world on Christmas Eve."

Dr. Robinson gave his name and number to the kids on behalf of himself and The Patient.

The kids curtsied, thanked the men and promptly pranced their way back inside the hospital with those bald heads seeming to cast a faintly glimmering halo around their heads as they stepped inside the well-lighted hospital atrium.

Dr. Robinson and his patient looked at each other.

"You had a question," The Patient prompted.

"A question?" asked Dr. Robinson, blinking again, the motorcyclist now struggling to make his way out of the highway swimming pool, dripping wet, but back on dry ground.

"Yes, you asked me about the ten billion and the ten just before the cookie girls ambushed us."

"Yes...yes indeed!" exclaimed Dr. Robinson. "So, who are the ten billion? Or better yet, who are the ten?"

"Everyone," said The Patient quietly, looking off into space as if he was lost in pursuit of an elusive private thought of his own.

"Everyone? What do you mean everyone?" asked Dr. Robinson, almost indignantly as if he was personally affronted by the impossible mathematics of The Patient's offhand remark. "How can everyone be the ten, and also be the ten billion?"

"Easy. Most human beings, for every ten good thoughts, words or deeds they project, they soil the world with ten billion evil thoughts, words and deeds. So, everyone contains the ten good and ten billion evils within his or her own person."

"I see," said Dr. Robinson, looking lost in thought, now pursuing an elusive idea of his own.

"But I catch the drift of your initial question; you wish me to identify individuals who, I believe, have embodied all good versus the ten billion others," said The Patient, his eyes hardening as if to capture not just Dr. Robinson's attention, but the man's very soul. "I can very easily give you a list of ten people who have embodied goodness at its highest and purest."

"Please," said Dr. Robinson.

"Jesus the Essene, Harriet Tubman, Prophet Muhammed, Muhammed Ali, Walter Payton, Arthur Ashe, Malcolm X, Sarah Moore Grimke, Fred Hampton, John Brown, Fela Anikulapo-Kuti, Bob Marley, Martin Luther King, Jr, Sojourner Truth, Saint Therese of Lisieux, Marcus Garvey, John Marks Templeton, and Howard Zinn. There are very many others, of course, I'm sure. But, these names simply are the first few to come to mind right now."

"You listed more than ten," said Dr. Robinson.

"So? I am asymmetric," The Patient retorted.

"And John Brown was white."

"I never claimed that all the pure souls were Black. You noticed I also included Zinn, Templeton, Therese, and, Grimke. There are so very many others; Black, white, Middle Eastern, Near East Asians, Far East Asians, Native Americans, Latinos, Latinas, you name it. Every ethnicity is blessed with a sprinkling of pure souls. The rest of the masses are kind of a leavening element."

"So, you're just going to blow up all these pure souls together with the rest of us?"

"Collateral damage," The Patient responded without mercy.

Dr. Robinson and The Patient noticed a spontaneous crowd clustering outside the hospital entrance. Doctors, nurses, custodians, patients, kitchen staff – people were talking and thumbing their cellphones at the same time.

"Something is going on inside the hospital," said Dr. Robinson, glancing at the swelling crowds. "I need to go see what this is all about."

"Save yourself the hassle. It's not inside the hospital," said The Patient; "I can tell you what's going on."

"Well…what is it?" Dr. Robinson snapped, and immediately looked startled by and regretful of his own tone. "What is happening?"

"The Statue of Liberty is gone," The Patient responded nonchalantly.

"What do you mean, 'the Statue of Liberty is gone'?"

"Poof. Gone. Disappeared. Dematerialized. Ghosted. The first domino has fallen!"

"But why?" asked Dr. Robinson plaintively.

"Why what?" The Patient teased.

"Why now? You promised a 24-hour grace period before…" Dr. Robinson continued to walk toward the gathering crowds.

"Promises, Dr. Robinson, are the most fragile things in this world; they get broken all the time. Besides, the Art of War is painted with brushstrokes of surprise. Unpredictability.

Stochastics. Asymmetrics."

"So, all those buildings, all those monuments, you're just going to up and blow them up?"

"Yes."

"But you gave people 24 hours."

"I lied. Sue me," The Patient stated as his face became an emotionless slab of black marble.

Dr. Robinson paused in his tracks and took what must be his first full measure of this strange man, this villain, this monomaniacal sociopath.

"By the time we reach the entrance to your hospital, Dr. Robinson, the White House will be history." said The Patient. "If we hurry, we can catch the first wave of that crowd's reaction to the next news." The Patient concluded turning to walk purposefully toward the milling crowds. Dr. Robinson, at a loss for words, gathered his wits and tagged alongside The Patient.

"Oh my God!" said someone in the midst of one of the pools of people. The speaker's voice sounded strangely strained as everyone turned in her direction. She was holding her cellphone up in her left hand and while covering her mouth with her right.

She was a nurse Dr. Robinson knew very well. Not a woman given to hysterics.

Dr. Robinson and The Patient made a bee line through the crowd toward the nurse.

"What's going on Ariel?" Dr. Robinson asked the nurse who was trying not to scream.

"I don't know, Dr. Robinson," said Nurse Ariel. "First, it was the Statue of Liberty, now Twitter is showing images of…of nothing…where the White House used to be. Doc, they say there's only some weird shimmering waves and dead silence at 1600 Pennsylvania Avenue…Excuse me Doc. I need to call my mom." The nurse stepped away from the crowd thumbing her phone.

"We need to talk," said Dr. Robinson to The Patient. "We really need to talk."

"I'm all ears," said The Patient.

"No. Not here. In my office. Now!" said Dr. Robinson, trying to assume some measure of authority and control. He pivoted and headed inside the hospital building. The Patient followed in the doctor's wake. His face was as close to pity as it had ever looked. He felt sorry for the poor doctor. He felt sorry for all the civilizing workers of mankind who had labored so hard over millennia of mankind's history precisely for the purpose of domesticating the likes of him. And now about to fail. Woefully, and permanently. The Patient felt that Dr. Robinson deserved to be pitied for now trying to succeed where all the gods have already failed.

"Good luck, Doc!" The Patient uttered under his breath as he followed Dr. Robinson back inside the hospital complex.

The men entered Dr. Robinson's office. They had hardly taken their seats when Dr. Robinson unleashed his suppressed rage at The Patient.

"You sir," said Dr. Robinson, "are a sociopathic monster!"

"I need a second opinion," said The Patient unmoved.

"You are blowing up historic monuments, the Statue of Liberty, the White House…"

"False gods," said The Patient, managing to egg the doctor on, while sounding bored at the same time.

"False gods?!" Dr. Robinson was incredulous. "Did you just call the Statue of Liberty, the White House false gods?! These monuments of historic propor…"

"Save it, Doc," The Patient interrupted. "Please, save that canned crap for the sheeple."

"Are you calling the Statue of Liberty, the White House canned crap?!"

"Yes," said The Patient, "for lack of worse words. Doc, what do you really know about these so-called monuments?"

"It seems to me that I together with 7 billion other people all over the world know that the Statue of Liberty is a beacon of freedom and hope for all mankind, the tired, the poor, the humble masses yearning to breathe free…"

"Yeah, yeah, yeah," The Patient yawned. "Emma Lazarus and her New Colossus poem are pure pablum for poor plebeians! So, please can it, Doc! Your beloved beacon of hope – the Statue of Liberty – is nothing but the most massive monument ever constructed as a beacon to hypocrisy in the whole history of mankind!"

"Blasphemy!" Dr. Robinson spat, apoplectic with suppressed rage.

"A.K.A. the Truth," said The Patient..

"Support your charge!" Dr. Robinson ordered.

"We don't have time for this. But okay. Let us look at some of the data. When was the Statue of Liberty dedicated?"

"I don't know. But I'm sure you're going to tell me," answered Dr. Robinson.

"October 28, 1886," said The Patient, watching the psychiatrist jot down the information.

"Okay?" prompted Dr. Robinson.

"Not even a year after the dedication of your monument to national hypocrisy, in 1887, Florida became the first state to mandate segregated railroad cars. Florida was soon joined in that idiocy by Mississippi, Texas, Louisiana and other states. And thus, the Jim Crow madness which started in 1865 became official policy just one year after your beloved Statue of Liberty was dedicated." The Patient paused to assess the doctor's attention.

"Please…go on," urged Dr. Robinson pensively.

"And then on May 18, 1896 – less than a decade after the dedication of your great monument – the Supreme Court of the United States delivered its infamous Plessy versus Ferguson decision, thus giving the ultimate judicial stamp of approval to the United States of America's congenital mental illness: racism. They should have done us all a big favor at that point by changing the country's name to the United States of Hypocrisy. Of course, your less-than-Supreme Court -- even though the judges who worked there at the time would disagree with me on that categorization -- your muchless-than-Supreme Court was merely cementing its racist reputation that had been clearly established in 1857 in their decision on the Dred Scott case.

"Not until 1954 in Brown versus Board of Education did the Supreme Court acquire enough decency to undo the evil of Plessy versus Ferguson. 1954! Sixty-eight long years after the dedication of the Statue of Liberty!

"And let us not forget the racism suffered by Black service members during the World Wars. Men and women of color in the United States Armed Forces were relegated to second-class status in their armed forces even while laying down their lives fighting for the Jews who were being slaughtered by the Nazis in Europe and elsewhere. And wasn't the great Jackie Robinson of baseball fame court-martialed while he was in the U.S. Army? And for what? For refusing to go to the back of a segregated bus! Where was your Statue of Liberty then?!

"Where was your Statue of Liberty in August, 1955 when 14-year-old Black Emmett Till was beaten, shot and thrown into a river by two physically-grown, but mentally-andspiritually retarded Southern white men?

"Where, pray, was your Statue of Liberty in 1955 when Rosa Parks was waiting for Lady Liberty to come change the minds of retarded bus drivers in Montgomery, Alabama?

"Your Statue of Liberty stood her ground while some good old white men bombed the 16th Street Baptist Church in Birmingham, Alabama killing four little girls inside the church. That was 1963, eleven days after the US government had ordered integration of Alabama schools.

"Where was the Statue of Liberty when Americans of Japanese ancestry were thrown in concentration camps right here inside the so-called United States of America?

"This same Statue of Liberty also stood in dignified idleness even as John F. Kennedy – an Irish-American Catholic President was assassinated three years after he came into office on a promise of Civil Rights Reform.

"The Statue never served as a reminder to anyone to stop the bombing of Black neighborhoods in Tulsa, Oklahoma in 1921.

"The statue broke no sweat while Mississippi burned in the summer of 1964, or when Black grandmothers were being maimed and killed by law enforcement hooligans in Selma and Montgomery, Alabama in 1965.

"Your famous statue continued to promise freedom in February 1965, when one of the greatest flowers of mankind -- not just Black American manhood --one of the greatest flowers of all mankind, by the name of Malcolm X was gunned down literally under the feet of your idol – your great Statue of Liberty. All because the man had the audacity to not merely demand, but to command freedom and to display bravery for himself and for his people in the land of the free and the home of the brave. As I have said, the country should have been christened the United States of Hypocrisy.

"And need I remind you that in this same land of the free, this home of the brave, the Reverend Dr. Martin Luther King, Jr. was assassinated for daring to be brave enough to still love those who would deny him his freedom and humanity.

"Dr. King was gunned down less than 200 miles from the headquarters of the KKK, which is located in Pulaski, Tennessee, a town less than 1000 miles from the Statue of Liberty!

"And let us not forget that in your sweet land of liberty your FBI implemented a destroy-or-kill mission against a whole cadre of Black leaders who dared to sue for their human rights. And yet in the very same nation, hoodlums are marching around with white hoods over their heads as they engage in acts of domestic terrorism. But the FBI never saw fit to open a COINTELPRO mission against them.

"And guess what? All of what I just told you continues to take place to this day. The only difference is many members of the KKK have traded their white garb of idiocy for the better-tailored uniform of law enforcement. Same perennial evil, dressed in better fashion. And the FBI is now watering its racist roots by engaging in some evil program targeting what it calls Black Identity Extremists! No such program against White Identity Extremists though. The Hoover clan prefer to think of the KKK as some sort of benign Sunday School Society for gentlemen in white gowns who love to burn crosses, swear by Jesus, and throw bombs into Black churches.

"So, beyond Emmett Till, beyond the four little girls of the 16th Street Baptist Church, beyond Malcolm X, Martin Luther King, Fred Hampton, Huey P. Newton, Tupac Shakur, there are innumerable Michael Browns, Eric Garners, Atatiana Jeffersons, Breonna Taylors, Philando Castiles, Freddie Grays, Walter Scotts, George Floyds, Jacob Blakes, Tamir Rices, Ahmaud Arberys, Rayshard Brookses…And those are just the law enforcement victims. For every one of these killed by law enforcement, you should count 100 unknown victims killed by racist doctors in hospitals across this country. At least, unlike their law enforcement counterparts, the doctors have the decency to colorcoordinate their white coats to match the color of their KKK garb. That colorcoordination? Not so much on the part of law enforcement or judges. Anyway, this country reeks of all forms of systemic racism and apartheid, including medical apartheid. And, so I ask you this: Exactly whose liberty has that ridiculous statue been symbolizing since its dedication in 1886?"

"If you put it like that…" Dr. Robinson began.

"I'm not done yet!" The Patient snapped, showing a sign of human emotion for the first time since he entered the hospital. "I'm not done yet." He repeated in a softer tone, as if in apology for his sharp tone toward the doctor. "Tell me doctor, who gave America that statue?"

"The French people," answered Dr. Robinson.

"That's correct. But have you read up on how France tried so desperately -- and failed woefully -- to enslave Blacks in Haiti?"

"Sorry, I can't say that I'm up to speed on that," said Dr. Robinson

"Well, let me be the first to tell you that the same people who gave you your Statue of Liberty once had as their emperor a cretinous madman who should be in the Guinness Book of Records for having the greatest inferiority complex in the world. You may know him as Napoleon Bonaparte. The only thing the man possessed in greater measure than his military genius was his hatred of humanity -- especially the Black variety."

"So, what has Napoleon got to do with Haiti or the Statue of Liberty?" Dr. Robinson asked.

"Three European empires -- Spanish, British, and French -- were all roundly defeated by the Black freedom fighters of Haiti. On behalf of France, Napoleon threw everything he had at that little island nation. To no avail. Regular Black guerrilla fighters kept pounding the so-called greatest military genius of Europe, until the latter turned tail. Napoleon almost had a stroke over the matter -- ending up in exile -- and hating Haiti to the end of his pathetic little life. But my point is he was so furious with the old French slave colony, that he imposed a ruinous economic reparation sanction on Haiti that still bleeds that great warriors' nation dry to this day. So, if you think about it, here is a country -- France -- collecting war reparations funds from Haiti since 1804 until recently, and yet all that Haiti ever wanted was its freedom. And yet the very same country that is extracting whitemail money from Haiti because the latter dared to fight for its freedom…that very same county, France, then presents a Statue of Liberty free of charge to a nation where the very Supreme Court has been busy endorsing anything but human liberty! To really show you how messed up your world is, would you believe that both France and Haiti share the same national motto: Liberte, Egalite, Fraternite! Liberty, Equality, Fraternity! One country has tried to live by that motto; the other has consistently betrayed it. And of course, it is the very one that has betrayed its own motto that has also presented the world's greatest hypocrite nation with a Statue of Liberty!" The Patient paused, his eyebrows cocked askance, as if to ask Dr. Robinson if the good doctor was tracking the story line.

Dr. Robinson's eyes narrowed as if he was trying to focus all of his brain power on his patient's narrative.

"Please, go on, "Dr. Robinson urged quietly.

"There's more. Way more. Evil is infinite in all its variety. But we simply do not have the luxury of time. My question to you is, do you concede the possibility that this statue is…was a symbol of mockery and hypocrisy?"

"I can begin to see where you're coming from. But still…" Dr. Robinson let the sentence hang in the air.

The Patient kept looking at the clock located above the door frame. "It's now nine O'clock,"

"Why do you say nine O'clock? It's obviously four O'clock," said Dr. Robinson.

"It's now nine O'clock in London. Five hours ahead. Buckingham Palace is no more,``said The Patient.

"Jesus!" exclaimed Dr. Robinson.

'Guess what? That is the name of the ship used by Queen Elizabeth I, a former inhabitant of Buckingham Palace to transport slaves from West Africa to the so-called New World," said The Patient.

"What the hell are you talking about, man?" the doctor was losing the last vestiges of his professional neutrality.

"I'm talking about the so-called good ship named 'Jesus', which the rapacious Queen Elizabeth used to transport slaves out of West Africa to the New World in 1562."

"Look, man, I hate to say this, but I think you're getting more delusional by the minute," said Dr. Robinson. "I think you're spinning and inventing data just to support your diabolical scheme…A ship named 'Jesus'! You really expect me to believe that?"

The Patient did not respond. He just kept looking at Dr. Robinson as if he couldn't care less one way or another what the man chose to believe.

"First the Statue of Liberty, then the White House and now Buckingham Palace! How many people have you killed blowing these monuments up?!"

"How many people did they kill during that African Holocaust called slave trade?" The Patient retorted. "I'm guessing no one really knows for sure. But I've heard the number 24 million thrown around. So, I'm thinking okay, let's say 24 million Africans were stolen and they died -- were killed -- in and by a life of slavery."

"So, now, you kill people who never enslaved those 24 million Africans?"

"I wish I did. And in twelve days from now, I'll kill everyone anyway. But in fact, for now, the occupants of the White House and Buckingham Palace should be safe. But if any of the inhabitants of those dens of evil had any common sense, they would have evacuated by last week. But surely, they have all evacuated before now."

"Evacuated by last week? You gave people just a few hours of warning," Dr. Robinson pointed out.

"No. All the target buildings received their countdown warnings on their computers every day for the past three weeks. I sent them time-release messages through QuantumTor daily. So, I know for a fact that those buildings should have been empty for more than two weeks now."

"QuantumTor? What is that? What the hell are you talking about?" Dr, Robinson asked, letting his exasperation flow freely.

"Dr. Robinson, QuantumTor is very much above and beyond your pay grade," The Patient replied, his face impassive and implacable like a steel vault door.

"So, all these VIP's have evacuated?"

"There are no longer any VIP's in the world," retorted The Patient, sounding annoyed. "I have made that stupid, arrogant little term permanently obsolete. But yes, the former occupants of the Dens-of-Thieves should have evacuated by last week."

"Where to? Do you know?"

"I know everything – Or, rather I'm plugged into Gorgon Brain – the global machine brain that sees and hears and knows everything."

"Gorgon Brain?"

"Sorry, Doc -- that's another tool way above your pay grade,".

"So, where are all these people now?"

"Exactly where I want them to be."

"Which is where?"

"A place code-named Noah's Ark, which is the most classified version of the more public Raven Rock and the rest of the Relocation Arc."

"Good God!" said Dr. Robinson.

"I beg to differ," said The Patient as he guffawed at his own semi-joke.

"But why?" Dr. Robinson asked, again plaintively.

"Why what, doctor?"

"Why me? Why you? Why this? Why now? Why Everything?"

"Why everything?" The Patient echoed, tasting the words. "I like that question, 'why everything?' Doctor, I think you're now finally ready to engage. So, let's find out 'why everything.' Shall we?"

"So you really do want to destroy the world?"

"Destroy the world??" The Patient asked, feigning indignation. "Hell no! I don't want to destroy the world; I'mma delete it. Permanently."

"So, all the civilization, the history, the grand tapestry of human achievements…you're just going to, how do you say it, delete all of it just like that?"

"Yes," said The Patient, refusing to be baited into making a case for or justifying or apologizing for his mission.

"You know, President Abraham Lincoln once expressed a profound sense of hope that the government of the people, by the people, for the people, shall not perish from the Earth," intoned Dr. Robinson in the manner of one reciting an incantation.

"Lincoln's error, Dr. Robinson, was in his mistaken belief that such a government already existed on Earth in the first place," said The Patient. "Perhaps, his statement was a self-congratulatory reference to what he imagined the United States to be. First of all, America -- the very busy-body nation that struts all over the world bullying other countries to practice democracy is one of the most undemocratic nations in the world. We keep plucking undemocratic specks out of other nations' eyes, while always sporting a big old log jutting out of our own eyes. We have become a colossal embarrassment to ourselves. And it is precisely our potential which is so great that makes our abysmal performance that much more embarrassing! We climb to the rooftops of the world, and make all these great rooster noises about China, and Russia, and Iran and North Korea, and any other country that dares to tell us to go screw ourselves; in the meantime, we perpetrate the most heinous atrocities at home and abroad in the most undemocratic ways possible. We, in the military, are constantly being abused and misused…we are constantly deployed to fight stupid foreign wars for the sake of grabbing from other countries their oil, their tin and their rubber. Nothing we have is ever enough. We are permanently hungry for more. We destabilize nations left, right and center in order to separate them from their natural resources. We set neighboring nations against one another just so we will always win unsustainable commercial wars, and to hell with everyone else. We willfully destroy and decimate the world, as if there is a planet B reserved for us Americans to escape to when this one is done serving our purpose. We behave as if everything -- including our fragile little planet -- is disposable! We have no national integrity, no moral ethos. The only thing we worship is money. And we never hesitate to offer up our own citizenry as well as foreigners as human sacrifice in our monomaniacal devotion to the Almighty Dollar. And then, we turn around and try to deal to others the duplicitous drug of American democracy. We have always been a great and busy nation. We constantly busy ourselves with gorging, drinking, ogling and cheering. Bread, and bloody circus; that's all we know; that's all we are programmed to want. And of course, with the passage of time, we have become a greater and busier nation just so we could avoid engaging in the much harder task of becoming a good nation. And so, in the mad rush to be great, America has woefully failed to be good. And unfortunately, as America goes, so goes the rest of the world. We have built a planet of lemmings and mad pigs! And so I will not merely run us all off the cliff, I shall blow up the whole rotten rock!"

"Good God, man! You've got to be some kind of Commie to hate our democracy so!" The veins on Dr. Robinson's neck bulged.

"Your democracy, eh?" The Patient asked. "You want to know my definition of your democracy?"

"I'm sure you're going to tell me," said Dr. Robinson.

"No, I won't. Not unless you invite me to tell you."

"Alright, fine," Dr. Robinson conceded. "Please, pray tell."

"Very well, I define your much-vaunted democracy as the government of the sheeple, by the weasels, for the vultures."

"My God!" Dr. Robinson looked aghast. "How cynical, how sociopathic can you get?!"

"And do you know what the weakest link in that chain is?"

"What?" Dr. Robinson asked.

"The sheeple!' The Patient remarked. "If you wipe out the sheeple, the weasels would devour one another. Then the vultures will gorge on the carcasses of the sheeple and the weasels until there is no more carcass-food. Then the vultures will face mass-extinction due to starvation. This will end your democracy.

"The only problem with that plan is I have run out of patience. I happen to believe that the whole intricate network of systems is infinitely complex, and that almost everyone has the sheeple, the weasel and the vulture inside their own soul. And so, my solution is to take out everyone at once. We all go meet Jesus at the same time. And we let God sort out his own divine list of who's who!"

"My God!" said Dr. Robinson matter-of-factly. "You really are a madman."

The Patient just kept looking at the psychiatrist as at a child who was celebrating his newly acquired knowledge of the fact that two plus two would always equal four.

"Alright," said Dr. Robinson. "Just tell me! How can I help put a stop to this madness?"

The irony of the question was not lost on The Patient. "Dr. Robinson, you had asked earlier: "Why me? Why you? Why this? Why now? Why everything?"

"Yes, I did ask that," admitted Dr. Robinson.

"Well, I think if we pursue those lines of inquiry, the answer will emerge as to how you can stop what you so – shall we say – professionally termed 'this madness'."

"Okay, yes, please tell me why all this?"

"Alright, Doc, in the interest of time, I'll summarize it all for you as best as I can." said The Patient.

"I'm listening," said Dr. Robinson.

"The whole history of humanity and it's opposite – inhumanity – can be summed up in six words: divide and conquer; unite and control! But if you prefer a less verbose summary, then I'll give you a three-word summary of the whole shebang: Dehumanize and dominate!"

"Please explain," Dr. Robinson prompted.

"I will," said The Patient. "Just try to follow along as best you can. I'll break it down into those five questions you had asked: Why me? Why you? Why this? Why now? Why everything? And as a bonus I will tell you how I'm going to do it, and what I expect will happen after I'm done blowing your planet up."

I was born in Oakland, California, one of two twin-boys of a Black couple. My mother was a member of the Oakland Chapter of the Black Panther Party.

My father was an African prince. His name was Olorogun Ashipa Ado Gabaro. He had traveled to America from a very advanced but well-hidden nation located right in the very heart of Africa.

Although my father had been sent by his father -- the king -- on a mission of reconnaissance to simply observe and record the ways of the "primitive, but arrogant" Americans, my dad had developed radically revolutionary ideas of his own, some of which they said had been sparked by his initial contacts with the extremely racist police in Oakland at the time.

Following his initial run-ins with the police, my dad had become interested in the Black Panther Party for Self-Defense.

It was at a Panther outreach program that he had met my mom, a University of California student-activist named Nzingha Fatiman.

My parents fell in love at first sight. They eloped and got married.

Within a couple of years, their marriage was blessed with the arrival of twin boys – my brother Eric and I.

My parents -- according to my mom -- agreed on everything except one: whom to fight for.

My father had insisted on raising us to become warriors who would fight to emancipate all Black people everywhere in the world.

My mom had disagreed with him.

She had insisted – like a true Black Panther Party member – that we must fight for all oppressed people everywhere. All oppressed people regardless of color, ethnicity, gender, religion, you name it. Black, white, yellow, red, brown, gay, lesbian, Trans, male, female, young, old, muslim, Christian, you name it. It didn't matter one bit to my mom.

As far as she was concerned, all underdogs – not just Black underdogs, all underdogs everywhere had to be emancipated.

They reached an impasse, a checkmate, and neither would give an inch.

My mother eventually settled on a heartbreaking King Solomon solution: split the child!

Thankfully, they had not one, but two kids to split.

They wrote our names on two strips of paper, and placed the strips, all balled up in a jar.

They drew lots. Only one of them had to pick a name as the unpicked name would automatically belong to the other parent.

As I already said, that singular parental decision may have unhinged both of my parents.

In any case, the two semi-families went our separate ways. But it also turned out each parent was keeping tabs on the other twin and the ex.

I met my twin – for the first time, consciously – on the night my father was assassinated.

Next day, my mom grabbed Eric and me and fled with us to Haiti, the Black republic that had conquered Spain, Britain and Napoleon's France, and had in victory still been magnanimous enough to declare that the Polish and German whites who were left in the country after Napoleon had turned tail, that those whites would be automatically considered Blacks according to Haiti's constitution, and would therefore enjoy all of the same freedoms and privileges guaranteed to the Blacks by the Haitian Constitution.

But raising two rambunctious boys single-handed was beginning to prove too much even for my very tough mother.

She turned to alcohol. She hit the bottle with the same force she attacked everything else: full frontal assault.

Next thing we knew, Eric and I were conducting nightly search and rescue missions in the most dangerous sections of Port Au Prince, half carrying, half dragging our mom home every night.

Two years went by.

One day -- a Sunday -- she woke up with the shakes. She looked terrible. She said she felt terrible. Throwing up and down. Delirium tremens, she said!

Then she reached for her last bottle of Vodka, and poured it straight down the toilet, wretched some more, and flushed.

I'll never forget it. Even as the toilet was still gurgling in the background, she called us, and told us to get dressed; we were going to church.

We marched, all three of us -- each trembling, each one for different reasons -- all the way to our local church.

Eric trembled, fearing that his fellow gang-members would spot him going to church.

I trembled because I was afraid my classmates would find out I did not have the perfect all-American family I had told them all about.

And my mom – my mom just simply trembled from her delirium tremens..

Somehow, we made it to the church.

One look at my mom's condition, and the usher refused to let us in.

Mom insisted that the usher call the pastor – a friend of hers.

The pastor came to the door to see what the commotion was all about. He took one look at my mom's condition, and uttered one word: "Sorry!"

He then whispered in the usher's ear, and the latter ever so gently closed the door in our faces. We were left outside, staring at the closed door of our local church.

We turned around, and marched back home, each of us still trembling – but now from a different kind of emotion: rage.

For the next four days, my mom suffered terribly, forcing herself to cold-detox.

Eric and I dared not go to school for fear we would come home from school to find her dead.

By Wednesday night, the old Nzingha had returned. The very next day, she took us to the airport and bought three one-way tickets from what is now known as the Toussaint Louverture International Airport in Port Au Prince straight to New York.

We arrived at JFK International Airport on Friday morning. And from there, we took a taxi straight to Mosque #7 in Harlem, New York.

I found out much later that in joining that particular Masjid, my mom secured four things:

1) Her sobriety,

2) A 'family' of sober-minded individuals to help her raise two rambunctious boys,

3) A teaching position at the Masjid's school, and

4) A home city that is the capital of all the world's good and evil. A city she could use just by driving us around every weekend and pointing out things to show us all of the various faces of good and evil, and how the world is played like a ballgame between the two teams of humanity.

As members of the great New York Masjid, my mother, my brother and I were given the opportunity to change our names.

My brother kept his: Eric Stevens.

My mom changed her name from Nzingha Fatiman to Sanite Belair.

And I changed mine from Derrick Olorogun Stevens to Black Messiah Justice. Yes, I changed my first name to Black, my middle name to Messiah, and my last name to Justice. I had actually wanted my last name to be Messiah, but our Imam told me that as a Muslim, I would be required to use the correct Arabic translation. So my name would have been Black Masih or Black Al-Masih. I told him and my mom that it sounded too much like 'mercy' to my pre-teen ears, and mercy was not an emotion I thought I could ever feel for the enemies of my people! So, we compromised: they asked me to move the Messiah to the middle, and suggested I adopt Justice as my last name. Black Justice. I loved it...I still love it. So, we officially changed my name from Derrick Olorogun Stevens to Black Messiah Justice. Go ahead, laugh!

Why? You wanna know why I chose that particular name? Why do you suppose I chose it? Yes, yes, I know it sounds like the name of a comic-strip superhero. Well, as a psychiatrist, you should be able to imagine my state of mind: coming of age, running from country to country, powerless, trying to face the world with only my mom, my brother and our Masjid as allies...and most of all, my mom had just then taught us about something called COINTELPRO, an FBI counterintelligence program directive put out by J. Edgar Hoover that had several goals, one of which was specifically to prevent what he called the rise of a Black Messiah.

No, I'm not kidding, Doc. Google it. COINTELPRO. Yes. That's the name of the program. And it involved discrediting and or killing potential Black leaders.

So, naturally, as a kid raging through the throes of puberty and all what-not, I chose the most powerful name I could think of. And right there and then, I pledged to my mother and our Imam that I would grow up to be that Black Messiah, the rise of whom the evil Edgar Hoover struggled so hard to prevent.

Seriously. True story. Now you know my real name. Not that it matters at this point, anyway. And as I have told you, because of my work for Uncle Sam, I've had more names than I can sit here and recall.

So, my real name is Black Justice. Nickname: BJ. Call sign: Rogue1.

Anyway, that's all neither here nor there.

The next thing we knew, my mom proceeded to put us through an educational crucible that was designed to either break us down, or else build us up spiritually, mentally and physically to the point where Eric and I became completely immune to all forms of fear.

She taught us two parallel subject streams; one set for us to ace government-sanctioned public tests, and another set which she referred to as our real education.

Our real education focused mostly on real history -- stuff she called the well-hidden history of the eternal war between the forces of good and the forces of evil in this world. And she never failed to point out real examples to us on the news and in our day-to-day lives.

The three of us became such a pain to the librarians of the New York library system that rumor had it they threw a block party when my brother and I gained admission to Annapolis and West Point respectively, so desperate were they to see us leave town for a while, at least.

We both graduated from our respective colleges at age 19.

After that, we both did our doctoral work at MIT, Eric in Material Science, and I in what my professors and I used to call 'Queasy'. The actual thing I did was officially called Quantum Weaponization/Artificial Intelligence/Systems Engineering. QWAISE. Yeah. Or QUEASY, as my faculty advisors referred to it.

The important thing was that both the theory and the applied engineering aspects of my thesis were so far from mainstream thought, that DARPA had no idea what to make of it; whether to classify or not to classify it. Eventually, the powers-that-be at the time decided that my thesis was so abstruse that it essentially classified itself, since it seemed that I was the only one in the world who could make any sense of what I wrote. DOD closed my file. MIT gave me my PhDs, and off I went to the Army to try qualify for Delta Force, while my twin took off to be a Navy SEAL.

His research at MIT had revolved around some exotic material he had once told me about when we were kids in New York. He had also insisted that there was a secret super-advanced nation in the depths of Africa and that his exotic material could be found only within the mountains of that secret nation.

At the time, I had figured that my brother was delusional, especially when he told me that our dad had been a prince from that secret nation. And that he had been killed by our uncle -- the king -- for sharing the secret material with outsiders.

Then I had thought -- I had 'known' -- for sure that Eric had lost his mind, probably due to the trauma of losing our dad. Since I had always been raised by Mom, I hadn't felt dad's loss that bad.

Anyway, Eric became a SEAL, eventually making it into DEVGRU, and I eventually became a member of the Unit.

The Unit?

Yes, Delta. That's right: Delta Force. Yeah, 'The Unit' is one of our nicknames. Doesn't matter.

So, anyway, Eric and I were both in Tier-One Elite military teams.

Next thing you know, we both made JSOC.

JSOC? Joint Special Operations Command. We were both based in North Carolina.

And our mom had moved to Atlanta, your great city here in Georgia.

Next thing I knew, I received a call from mom. I could tell from her voice something was very wrong, but she was still trying to shield me from whatever it was. I was thinking maybe cancer, terminal diagnosis, something. I made the trip from base to Atlanta in under five hours.

Yes, I went to see her. She broke down and told me that my twin brother had just died fighting for the throne of that same mysterious nation Eric used to tell me all about.

Then, for the first time, my mom revealed all she knew about my dad's real background. Which I later learned was much more than even she or Eric ever knew.

But that's a story for another day.

Fast forward to the war three years ago.

Still classified location, which really doesn't matter now, one way or another. But anyway, we were behind enemy lines, all eight of us, way deep inside hostile territory, I was leading what we all knew was pretty much a suicide mission. We were to penetrate this specific nuke-enriching facility, and insert malware into an air-gap computer. The idea was to effectively short-circuit this particular nation's nuclear launch capabilities so that the nukes would instantly detonate right inside their own borders as soon as they are launched. No need to engage them with SDI. What? What's SDI? Strategic Defense Initiative…you know: Star Wars. No, not the movie, the military anti-nuke program. You know what? It really doesn't matter. Just forget I mentioned any of those details.

Anyway, as I was saying, there were eight of us – all JSOC ghosts, five Blacks, two Latinos, and one white guy -- all war dogs, each one trained to bring a whole country down, by any means necessary.

Seven of us -- including myself -- were regular JSOC ghosts. And then there was DJ Tate, who was a last-minute surprise insertion into our team. None of us knew his military background. All we knew was that he was the President's son, and he was now officially our eighth man. Moreover, I was told in no uncertain terms that it had become my job to bring him home safely at all costs. Crazy mission. Suicidal as all get-out. Yet, somehow, not only must I survive, I was also responsible for the survival and safe delivery back state-side of the President's only son!

Yes. That's correct. The very same DJ Tate -- the President's son.

Anyway, for reasons unknown to me at the time, our mission went down smoothly. Too smoothly. Until it was time to exfil. Then all hell broke loose.

We had made it to the extraction point.

What? Didn't you learn to speak military during your hostage-negotiation career days? Well, okay. No big deal. Basically, an extraction point is a pre-designated spot where we all agreed to meet our helo -- our helicopter to extract us back to safety.

Next thing we knew instead of dropping a ladder for all eight of us to climb aboard, the pilot deployed a basket to lift up one person at a time! Made no damn sense. But we were trained to adapt instantly to any changing fog of war.

Without any discussion or debate, we all pointed to DJ, indicating that the President's son should go up first. Just one of those baked-in warrior ethos. Total BS, right? But we're…we were military, and that's how we were trained to roll. Honor code.

Strangely -- at the time -- DJ didn't even attempt to play the noblesse oblige card. He simply scrambled aboard that basket and got scooped up. And fast.

Then the shit hit the fan. Two grenades were dropped on us from the helo as the bird banked funny like it was maneuvering to gunship us to shreds.

We all dove on the grenades -- almost at the same time. All seven of us. But I beat them all to it. I was the one who landed directly on top of the grenades.

Six guys with heavy gear all landed on top of me. The grenades went off at the same time as the gunship mowed down my brothers.

What? Who?

Yeah, of course, they all died. Yes, right there on top of me.

Every one of us had tried to sacrifice our lives for the others by diving on top of the grenades. But I got there first. And that's why I'm here talking to you today. The other six piled on top of me. And because of it, they covered me from the gunship hailstorm.

I had to move real quick. But not before confirming what I already knew. All six were dead. Turned out the grenades I had dived on top to shield my guys from were not grenades at all, but flash-bangs designed to create confusion and disorientation. And possibly to call the enemies attention to our position.

So, diving first to save those men was what saved my life and caused them to lose theirs, as they too dived to save mine.

I was disoriented. Confused. Didn't know if DJ had been kidnapped by the enemy or rescued by our SOAR operators or what.

Everything had happened so fast. It was Oh Dark Thirty. After the gunship disappeared, everything had become eerily darker and more silent. I could hardly see anything through my NODs. But I could smell the garlic from Willy Pete. So, I knew...

What's what?

A NOD? A NOD is a Night Optical Device. And Willy Pete is white phosphorus. It has this unmistakable acrid, garlicky odor. Bottomline was I figured real quick that that bird was planning to light us up. It was the only reason I could think of for them to drop all their Willy on us. It smells like hell, and burns even worse when you light it up. That's why some call it the Devil's Element in the Periodic Table.

Long story short, I scrammed out of Dodge. And fast.

Did someone at the top decide to exfil only the President's son, and delete the rest of us? Was he kidnapped? If so, how could the kidnappers know that we would choose him to go up first? Wild guess? Dumb luck? Kidnapper psych 101? What? It was all coming down too strange, too fast, too surreal.

I had no time to wonder. I had to get out of the area. And make it to a safe place. But could I trust any government-sanctioned safe houses?

I decided not to trust anyone until I gathered more intel. So, I slipped off the grid. And became a ghost. Zero contact with my mom, my only family. I had no friends. And I considered all my former associates Opfor until further notice.

Opfor? Sorry…Opposing force. That is 'the enemy', as far as I was concerned. At least, until I got evidence to the contrary. So, for all practical purposes, during the following months, there was only one person I could trust in the whole world, and that was my mom. And I couldn't even contact her -- for her safety, and mine.

I became a professional ghost. Dropped totally off the grid. I eavesdropped on the world through QuantumTor. I lived off the land deep inside the Amazon jungle. All I needed were food, water and a military grade satellite computer connection. My hideout spot had plenty of food and clean water.

I used bitcoin to buy needed electronic parts from the city near my jungle. I built my own military-grade satellite computer, and generated my own electricity by hooking a DIY-turbine to a rushing stream.

Regular folks get their news from CNN.

Operators know that the best source of bombshells are bars and nightclubs. If you know how to hack bars, you'll be a god on Wall Street. All the news not fit to print can always be culled from certain bars sprinkled all over the world. You just need to know how to choose your bars and their internet channels, and how to hack your way in and have enough discipline to just lurk and listen.

Diplomats, generals and billionaires are birds of a feather. They tend to flock together. They and their assistants all patronize the same set of hangouts.

So, from my jungle spot, I scanned the diplomatic community's back channels until I hit pay-dirt.

It started with talk about DJ being a hero because of his valor during our clandestine mission.

First of all, our mission was highest priority classification. How did these loose lips get to hear and speak about it at a nightclub in Hong Kong?

Second of all, that titbit of gossip made me conclude that DJ in fact made it back home safe. That was a relief as I had promised the President's messenger that if only one of us returned home, I would make sure it was Junior. So, talk of heroism made me realize that for reasons yet unclear to me, I had somehow kept my word to the President.

Then the drumbeats started getting louder. It was two years ago, an election year, and there was talk that if DJ happened to be awarded a Medal of Honor for his heroic deeds, a second term of office would be all but practically guaranteed for President Richard Tate.

Heroism?! Medal of Honor?! Presidential Stakes??

Then it hit me: we had been set up. The mission. The selection of the operators. Even the extraction point and the timing of the extraction. The whole dance had been choreographed for just one purpose: to secure the re-election of President Richard Tate. Well the fool got re-elected alright. And the world has been a worse place for it. Even the idiots who rushed to re-elect him can't wait to get rid of him.

Yes, of course. I imagine you already know all that. Pardon me. Didn't mean to bore you with background political detail.

Still, that backstory launched the chain of events leading to my decision to end the world.

From my basecamp in the Amazon jungle, I began to put the pieces of the jigsaw puzzle together.

In so doing, I saw that the trail neither began nor ended at the White House. Turns out President Tate was just a mere puppet, an immoral and utterly brainless little puppet of master-manipulators, who in turn were having their own puppet-strings yanked by ever more highly placed and much grayer grise eminences.

I drew connections till I became dizzy. There were inner circles within inner circles within inner circles. A pure Gordian Knot if ever there ever was one. A royal spaghetti mess!

To say that I was flummoxed does not even begin to describe my state of mind.

Within it all, one question kept nagging at me like a tongue on a loose tooth: my mom.

How was she holding up? Along with the other parents, she had been at Dover Airport to watch the fake caskets rolled in.

The authorities had informed the seven families of our KIA status. The families would have all been briefed and prepped about the rituals, the ceremonies. Each family would be assigned their own handlers. Dover, Arlington, the whole nine yards.

The authorities prepped and rolled the seven caskets in at Dover.

But I already knew that they had a full-scale global manhunt for me. Through my listening posts in the back channels, I already knew that I was a dead man running. No safe-house would ever be safe enough for me.

Still, my mom. I was all she had left…and she had been led to believe that even I was KIA, although the authorities knew I had escaped.

One tradition she and I had shared over the years was her birthday. If I wasn't deployed or undergoing some deep cover training somewhere, I always arranged to be there for her birthdays. I had promised her, and I had always kept my promise by duly showing up and taking her out to eat at her favorite Caribbean restaurant in Atlanta. After that, we would usually binge-watch the Hidden Colors video series. And then she would nag me to death about her ambition of traveling the world with her bunch of non-existent grandkids and her future daughter-in-law whom I kept "failing to produce" on demand.

Funny, my mom was my Achilles heel. My mom and my word. Not keeping my word has always been my greatest fear. And not keeping my word to my mom was utterly unthinkable for me. I knew "they" were surveilling her. But my fear of being captured was no longer as strong as my fear of breaking a promise to my mom. I would show up for my mom's birthday. And we would have a good old time, even if we might need to skulk around under the cover of darkness or wear crazy disguises or something.

So, three weeks before my mom's birthday, while America was still enjoying the afterglow of Richard Tate's re-election, I packed up my gear and buried them right there in the jungle, just to cover my tracks and to travel light.

Bitcoin has been my American Express; I never leave home without it. And with it, I was able to hop, skip and jump from Brazil to Colombia to Haiti, and then to Miami.

Traveling with serial Ubers through the backroads, by about one week to my mom's birthday, I had made it to Savannah, Georgia.

Then all hell broke loose. Remember the story of the Black woman who launched an all-out assault on the White House on Christmas Day, two years ago.

Yes, I know there have been several of those since then. I'm talking about the very first one two years ago. On Christmas Day. I'm talking about the lady who used the swarm drones to paint that huge Black Panther graffiti, and wrote All Power to the People right on the very frontage of the White House.

And while the guards were scrambling to shoot down the drones without shooting into the White House, she launched RPGs at the White House from her armored van parked across the street, and live-streamed most of the assault.

The Secret Service had to rush Richard Tate down into the White House bunker. Word has the man soiled himself on the way down. Since then, the Secret Service's nickname for the President has been President BS: Bunker Stinker.

Patience, please Doc! I'm getting there! This is the one part of my story that will put everything in perspective for you.

Anyway, the bottomline is this: that one-woman army was my mom. Sanite Belair. Go on YouTube, TikTok or Twitter. Search for the footage of that assault. You'll notice "Sanite Belair 1804" tagged next to the left front paw of her Black Panther graffiti.

As a member of the Black Panther Party for Self-Defense, my mom had received some training in asymmetric warfare.

And as I had advanced through the ranks, I had added to her knowledge-base and skill-set. Basically, by the time she launched that attack on the White House, she had become one hell of a Black mother. Not the kind you wanted to cross, ever.

Anyway, she tagged and lit up the White House. And once they managed to extract their heads from their asses, the authorities returned fire. But she dominated the first few seconds of that firefight.

And guess what she did with that tactical advantage?

No. Just guess.

Okay, I'll tell you what she did. She used the sound of her shooting to send me a message. Three short bursts. A lapse. Then a single shot. Dot. Dot. Dot. Dash.

Dot. Dot. Dot. Dash. And then she repeated the pattern.

That's Morse Code for the letter V. Just like the opening bars of Beethoven's 5th Symphony, which became the Allied call sign during WWII.

It was our secret code, my mom and I. We had pre-arranged it as an emergency code to be used by either of us to signal to the other person to be vigilant or to vanish in case of extremely dire emergencies.

Mom and I had both been fans of V for Vendetta and I had long ago pre-arranged with her to use that V Morse Code as a sort of parting gift message to secure the other one's safety. Whether it be knocking on a door, blinking or breathing pattern or whistling or banging pots and pans together in the kitchen, that Morse Code pattern was to tell the other to V for Vamoose!

So, using the rhythm of her first few shots, my mom had contrived to send me one final message before they killed her; she told me to really V for Vanish.

Of course not, Doc. No one else knows about that message except me…And now you. And of course, too, at this point, it no longer matters whether anyone knows or not.

I was just telling you all this to give you some background.

Catch her? They didn't catch her; they killed her. The cowards unleashed so much firepower on that van, so much so that even the engine block melted inside that crater across the street from the White House.

One look at the site, and the experts immediately agreed that forensics were totally impossible.

So, the Army Corp of Engineers were called in to fill up the charred crater in front of the White House, to level it up, and rebuild the road as if nothing had happened there. As if to bury the evidence of my mom's crusade. She had discovered something. And whatever it was had pissed her off so much she had launched herself against the gods, and she had made gods tremble.

Like I said, never piss a Black off. Ever heard of Harriet Tubman?

Anyway, by New Year, the reconstruction of Pennsylvania Avenue had been completed. That road became level and smooth again, just as if nothing of import had happened there.

So, they killed and buried my mom in front of the White House. But they could never kill her spirit. Because she had used something called MagPi, DARPA-grade. MagPi? That's Magic-Angle graphene permanent ink. It's a kind of graphene-based paint that she used to spray-paint the Black Panther Party logo on the White House frontage.

And yes, they tried very hard to cover that graffiti with a million layers of white paint, but the white paint just wouldn't stick. Even the MagPi white paint couldn't cover the MagPi black paint up. The white paint is recessive -- like white genes. The black paint she used is dominant, so to speak. You know what they say about one drop of Black blood. I guess the same goes for black MagPi graphene paint.

Sanite Belair's masterpiece lived on on the very frontage of the White House, until I blew it all up. Even after Tate commissioned a silhouette painting of himself holding a Bible, and instructing them to paint that blasphemy in black over my mom's Black Panther, you could still see the glow of her Black Panther shining through the painting of Tate's Bible.

You know what they say: Black don't crack!

So anyway, after my mom's murder by Tate, the tyrant, I decided to end all tyranny forever.

Before making that decision, I had been a ghost; once I made the decision, I became...God.

Go ahead: laugh. You think I'm a megalomaniac. You need to quit being a shrink, and try being human so that you can listen without trying to slap labels on me at the same time.

Anyway, as a ghost, although I was invisible to the grid, I was also not in charge of the grid.

But as God, I was everywhere and nowhere. I was completely invisible to the global grid, but I had also pwned it. I had total and uncontested -- incontestable -- control of the global communication nexus. I had rootkit of not only the Gorgon Eye and Gorgon Ear, I had installed myself as the undisputed Emperor of the global Gorgon Brain -- the quantum singularity that controls all data flow all over the world.

What?

Yes. Yes, of course, there is such a thing as Gorgon Eye. And Gorgon Ear. And Echelon. And Gorgon Brain.

Well, Doc, why would you know anything about it? It has nothing to do with the human brain. No. The Gorgon Brain is the ultimate quantum AI entity that runs the world.

How did I know about it? What do you mean I'm just a soldier? Look, Doc; it really doesn't matter how I knew about it. But if you must know, I was the one who designed the nucleus algorithm for it. That was the essence of my doctoral thesis at MIT. And I was, and still am, the only one who fully understands its innermost working, its dialects and its nuance.

Bottomline is this: that all manner of petty tyrants, kings, prime ministers, emperors, presidents and Popes from the beginning of time have strained and struggled to rule the world. They have all failed.

But I, the son of a Black Panther...I have succeeded. Simply by pwning the one machine that rules the whole world.

The only problem the world now faces is I don't want to rule the world.

I have taken over the world for one and only one purpose: to burn it.

Why?

Because, as I already stated, I'm putting an end to all tyranny. You don't see the connection? Doc, have you ever treated a dead man? For anxiety? No? For depression? No? For sociopathy? No?

Well, that's my point exactly. My point is that when I blow up the world and we are all dead, there will be no more victims of tyranny...But neither will there be any more tyrants.

So, I have taken over the world in order to end the world. Tyranny will end because the world will end.

How? Once again, I'm telling you that I am a dead man's switch.

So, now, why you?

Because I have had unparalleled access to all of your hostage-negotiation work.

Top Secret Security Clearance? Please, don't make me laugh!

Think of my Security Clearance as Level-whatever-the-hell-I-choose-to-make-it. That is my Security Clearance Level.

Anyway, I know all about your hostage-negotiation works in the West Bank, in Afghanistan, in Nigeria, Somalia, Germany, South Korea-North Korea DMZ, Hong Kong, Washington DC, Ireland, Dubai, Istanbul, Mumbai, Beijing, Moscow...Want me to keep going?

Okay, good!

So, now, you have an opportunity to attempt the greatest hostage negotiation of all time. This could be your magnum opus! I am holding the world hostage, and you get to negotiate its release. You get to persuade me not to blow up the world together with its seven billion inhabitants.

And you have very limited time to do it. How much time? Well that depends on how fast your President Richard Tate and his cohort of petty tyrants respond to all my demands.

What?! What do you mean you don't care? You want to see seven, eight billion people die when it is within your power to try and save them, doctor?

You have pancreatic cancer? Six weeks max? Well, I'm sorry to hear that. I guess Gorgon missed that bit of detail about you. That was definitely not in your healthcare records.

You used old-school paper HIPAA?

Interesting! Now, this is becoming very interesting. So, you'll be dead in six weeks anyway? But as a doctor, you don't feel any impulse to save the world even as you yourself are dying of terminal cancer?

Eschatology? What the heck is that? And what's it got to do with saving the world?

The study of the end…interesting, really interesting hobby you've got there, Doc! A little morbid, if I'm allowed to say so myself. Eschatology…study of endings! Wow! Is that a shrink-type hobby thing, or that's just you?

Okay so, between the terminal cancer and your eschatology hobby, you don't care one way or another whether I blow up the world or not?

So, now, we have the perfect case of professional therapeutic neutrality. How nice!

This is actually turning out to be more exciting than I had anticipated.

Very well then, "Ave Imperator, morituri te salutamus!"

What?

Why does it matter to you now how I'm going to blow it up?

Scientific curiosity?

Very well, I can respect that. Why don't we just say that over the past two years, I've managed to rig up weapons in containers, each one no bigger than a laptop.

And each of those containers has enough explosive capacity to dwarf all the nuclear weapons in the world. Every single one of them.

No, they are not nuclear, Doc. They are made of stuff that makes nuclear weapons break out in cold sweat.

What is this, Doc? Some form of morbid curiosity, eschatology or a sneaky form of extreme hostage negotiation technique?

Alright, fine. I'll tell you how, not that it would do you or the world any damn good, or give any advantage to the tyrants either way anyway.

It's called Gamma Ray Bursts. No, forget Vibranite. That's my twin-brother's pet rock.

No. What I have in each of those hidden boxes will generate enough bang to dwarf the explosion of ten thousand suns. And I have dozens of them strategically hidden all over the world. I even managed to secure a phone-sized one inside the ISS.

Yeah, ISS, the International Space Station. You bet I'm serious. Dead serious.

Yes. Gamma Ray Bursts.

Blame it all on MIT. I had access to material info that had been discarded and mothballed by everyone, including DARPA.

That was the subject of my personal thesis. I never discussed it with anyone until now.

Yeah, I know I could have earned four PhDs while I was there…Three are more than enough for me.

Plus, I could have got myself killed by any number of governments or mega-corporations if they knew about the existence of what I knew.

No, thanks. No, I kept all that to myself until now.

What about it? Well, now, it's too late for anyone to threaten me or kill me for it. I have no living relatives. And as I have already told you, I am now a dead man's switch.

If I die, your whole world will explode.

If I'm in pain, your whole world will explode.

If I'm in a coma, your whole world will explode.

Basically, I've rigged the system up so that if I get stressed, the world will come to an instant and very violent end.

My death will mark the end of all humanity.

Why are you smiling, Doc?

Yeah?

So, you're thinking I am some kind of deranged megalomaniac.

I beg to differ. I prefer to think of myself as a man with nothing to gain and nothing to lose. They, the various petty tyrants of this world have stripped away from me all that have ever mattered to me, and with them gone, I'm also now rid of the very last vestige of interest in playing any further role in their endless games of world domination.

They've destroyed or killed everyone and everything that ever mattered to me. I was born into a world at war. I was raised as a warrior. The art of war is baked into my very bone marrow. War is all I've ever known. Warrior is all I've ever been. And it is only fitting that I should end my life in the final war. The only difference this time is I am not allowing others to set the rules of engagement. This time, I dictate all the rules.

Human history is congested with all manner of petty tyrants who consistently rig the rules of engagement in their own favor. This parade of tyrants continuously cranks the perpetual motion machine which they designed to keep the wretched of the earth continuously wretched.

Well, not any more! I'm having none of it. I'm ending their eternal reign of terror, they who are the ultimate terrorists. Now, let them learn what it feels like to be on the receiving end of the ultimate and final act of terror.

They killed my mother! Richard Tate, and his long line of tyrannical ancestors killed my mother!! Now, they all must scream, as they watch me kill Mother Earth and all of her children. This time, there will be no coffins, no caskets; no funerals, no burials; there will be no burial grounds, no memorials. There will be no memories of anyone by anyone. There will be no more planet Earth.

I will light up your planet, and for one nanosecond, your whole world will be nothing but one funeral pyre.

The world system is rigged. It can never be fixed. Sooner or later, someone has to blow it up.

I am that someone.

No more people.

Therefore, no more tyrants.

Now,   let   the   end   begin!

His voice sounded clear and calm coming through every connected speaker all over the world. Gorgon Brain activated the auto-translate language module for every region of the world, together with voice-activated override set-up and record for any language of choice.

"People of the world. Stay calm. My name is Dr. Randall Robinson. I am a psychiatrist and a hostage-rescue negotiator.

"The world has been kidnapped. I repeat: the world has been kidnapped.

"As soon as this message started to broadcast, governments all over the world have already started struggling to scramble their weapons systems. That is their traditional response to crises. That approach will not work this time. We are dealing with a very different set of factors this time around.

"People of the world, please insist that your leaders remain calm. Any sudden moves on their part will unleash a catastrophic sequence of events that can not be undone.

"The kidnapper wishes me to inform all governments that he has suspended all of your old rules of engagement. He tells me to warn you to not activate any weapons except the weapons of the heart and the soul!

"He instructed me to warn you that any country that launches any weapons during this hostage crisis will be punished instantly and without mercy.

"He warns that any attempt to trace, track or capture him will trigger a dead man's switch. He says -- and I now have very good reasons to believe -- that if he suffers any discomfort or distress, never mind death, the world will end instantaneously. Again, I have very good reason to believe him. This is all the message he has asked me to read to you now.

"He further asks you to stay tuned. In the meantime, as a psychiatrist, I urge you to use this crisis period to reflect on the meaning of your lives. If we make it through these harrowing times -- and I pray we do -- I hope everyone would have used the experience to figure out how to live a more meaningful life going forward. Good day or goodnight wherever you are."

Dr. Robinson ended the broadcast and turned to Black Justice who had been looking on placidly as the former read the script, and also added his own little shrink twist at the end.

"Now, what?" asked Dr. Robinson.

"Dinner," Justice answered calmly.

"Chemo…No appetite," Dr. Robinson countered.

"Alright. I'll go grab a bite. I'll be right back," said Justice, as he exited Dr. Robinson's office.

On his way back from the hospital cafeteria, Justice saw the cookie girls seated across from the central nursing station playing with Barbie dolls.

Justice kept moving, and then, he did a double-take taking another look at the kids. Same Barbie model, except one Barbie was white, the other black. But the handling was in reverse: the Black girl was playing with the white Barbie and the white girl was playing with the Black Barbie. Same game, cross-racial approach. *Interesting*, Justice thought.

Off to one side of the nursing station, a nurse and a pleasantly psychotic patient were haranguing each other.

"Why, Mr. Jimmy, why?" the nurse asked the man with a tone of mock exasperation, slapping her forehead to drive home the point.

"Why what, Ms. Valerie?" the man countered feigning ignorance and innocence.

"Why in the middle of all that we already got going on are you wearing a sock in your breast pocket, Mr. Jimmy?"

"Because I have a date tonight?" Jimmy replied beaming, satisfied with his cleverly oblique response to Valerie's query.

"You have a date tonight?" the nurse, Valerie, played along.

"A very hot date, Ms. Valerie! Sizzling!"

"Where is your date?" Valerie coaxed.

"Harry Belafonte Hotel, of course," said Jimmy, breaking out in song, "Day-o, Day-o... A beautiful bunch o'ripe banana; daylight come and me wan' go home. Hide the deadly black tarantula; daylight come and me wan' go home! Day, me say day-o!"

"Okay, okay, Mr. Jimmy, we get it! But why do you have a doggone sock hanging from your breast pocket?" Valerie persisted.

"Ms. Valerie...I just done told you: I have a hot..."

"Date tonight. Yes. We get that," continued Valerie patiently, "What I'm trying to figure out is why a sock in your breast pocket? Why not a handkerchief, Mr. Jimmy?"

Justice took a seat next to the cookie girls watching the girls and also listening to the back-and-forth conversation between Valerie and Jimmy.

"Why not, Ms. Valerie? Why shouldn't a sock be promoted to a place of honor above my heart? Socks work just as hard as -- if not harder than -- handkerchiefs. This is part the discrimination that permeates this rotten society. You all expect the lowly, downtrodden sock to know its place in the order of things, and to remain downtrodden forever. And whenever a self-respecting sock lifts itself up by its own nearby bootstrap, you all scream foul, or whisper affirmative action!" Jimmy was getting worked up. Before his psychotic break, the man had been an urbane, erudite professor of Sociology at the John Brown Institute in Philadelphia.

Valerie started showing signs of regretting her error of tipping the professor over into lecture mode. Her eyes scanned wildly for any escape route, but she was cornered. She knew her mistake was about to cost her at least 15 minutes of buttonhole lectures on the nuances and excruciating details of human-rights violations by everyone in the world --except, of course, the venerable old Professor James Greenlee, Jr. who considered himself a sociological Don Quixote, the last guardian of human rights on planet Earth.

Valerie found a chair, took a seat and resigned herself to her inevitable didactic punishment.

A couple of nurses nearby suddenly found some pressing matters that needed their immediate attention as they surreptitiously moved to the opposite end of the nursing station. Close enough to hear every word of Jimmy's lecture, but far enough not to be sucked into his energy-sapping black hole. Smiles well-hidden, they shuffled and stacked patients' charts in unnecessarily perfect order.

"Tell me about your dolls," Justice said to the cookie girls.

"This is Brenda," said the Black girl, holding up the white Barbie.

"And this is Brandee," said the white girl, holding up the Black Barbie.

"Brenda and Brandee," said Justice. "Nice names."

"Why, thank you!" the cookie girls chorused.

Silence. Smiles. Innocent little girl giggles. No words. Volumes spoken. Little girl language.

"Your turn," said the white girl. "What's your name?"

"Black. Black Justice"

"That's a super-cool name!" said the Black girl.

"Thank you. I get that a lot," Justice responded. "You guys' turn. What are your names?"

"Brenda," said the white girl.

"Brandee," said the Black girl.

"No, wait, those are your dolls' names." Justice confirmed. "What I'm asking is, what are your own names?"

"Those are our names," the girls chimed.

"I am Brandee," said the Black girl.

"And I am Brenda," said the white girl.

"We were born in the same hospital, on the same day. Seven hours apart," said Brandee "And I'm older than her."

Brenda stuck her tongue out, pushed her index fingers into her cheeks and made a rasping rude sound at her friend.

"Our moms were best friends," said Brenda, "so we are BFFs!"

"BFFs," Justice repeated. "What's BFFs?"

"Best Friends Forever!" Both girls chimed.

"You said your moms were best friends…not are best friends. What happened between them?"

The giggles vanished. Brandee's eyes misted. Brenda started to sob.

"Alright, ladies," one of the eavesdropping nurses hollered at the girls. "Time to go back to your unit. Let's go! Elevators or stairs?"

"Elevators!" cried both girls.

Smiles back in places. Giggles in tow. Childhood and innocence. Justice shook his head, and headed back to Dr. Robinson's office.

Justice did not knock. He let himself into Dr. Robinson's office. He did not sit.

"Dr. Robinson," Justice squeezed his words through gritted teeth, sounding like a man who just turned on a very primal switch in his brain. "Dr. Robinson. Go to sleep. Tomorrow I'm going to war. Against enemies who are addicted to victory.

Thing is I don't have to win; but I am not going to lose. See you here at 0300 hours. I will attack at dawn. Goodnight." He wheeled around and left the doctor's office.

Dr. Robinson opened his mouth as Justice shut the door.

"0300,"   Dr.   Robinson   said   to   the   door.   "Roger   that!"

"Clear Rushmore now! Today, that mountain will be raining rocks. I will do to your Presidents' faces what the Little Man of Europe did to the Great Sphinx of Giza. The four Presidents whose faces you've carved over sacred Native American land, all four Presidents were racists. One was an overt racist, another was the racist who publicly lambasted Blacks even while fathering a child with a 16-year old slave girl. And then you have the one who was your more discreet closet racist, and of course, you have your Brownville racist, all these hypocrites will get a nose job today," said the mechanical V-for-Vendetta voice over the airwaves, sounding like the voice made famous by the Anonymous group.

"I had a choice: exposure or revenge, Pinocchio or the Sphinx? Elongate their noses and reveal their various fibs, or cut off their noses like one of their kind did in Egypt. I chose revenge. These men need no further exposure because anyone with even a grade-school education can read up on all their collective sins. But you people have been so thoroughly brainwashed -- you have all been perfectly well-trained to call evil good, and to call good evil, so much so that you continue to worship the very tyrants whom you would not want anywhere near your own pre-teen daughters!

"I now begin your final lesson. This is the beginning of the end of your world. Get ready. Or don't. It doesn't matter one way or another to me. Clear Mount Rushmore. And for what it's worth, try to enjoy the show."

The voice stopped. For a brief moment following the announcement, primordial silence reigned upon Earth. All human activities and their usual busy-ness froze. Even jungle animals sheltered in place because of the eerie silence. The animals had become so used to background human din, and the rumblings of machines doing human's work, that even they, the animals were terrified by the global silence, as the world stood still and held its breath.

And then came the chaos! The avalanche of noise.

The roar of the markets took on a blood-curdling edge starting in New Zealand.

The crash followed a jagged fault line along the world's major financial centers. The tectonic plates of big money shifted from New Zealand to Sydney, to Tokyo, then to Hong Kong and Singapore, and Mumbai and then Moscow.

Bleary-eyed Europeans became the next to awaken to the news of world devastation, and their own overnight state of destitution from Zurich to Frankfurt and London.

By the time the markets opened on Wall Street, the financial world had all but collapsed.

Chicago provided the coup de grace.

It took just one madman giving a nose job to the denizens of Mount Rushmore to make the markets crash.

Never before had the bulls been so violently castrated so expeditiously.

The billionaires called the Presidents. The Presidents called their Generals. And the masses called on their gods.

All the animals were now fully awakened; the Dragons, the Bears, the Lions and the Eagles were all flames and fangs, teeth and talons spoiling for a fight, roaring for a kill-fest. The Bulls had by then been bled dry. They had no fight left in them.

Before this was over, someone was going to die a million deaths -- one for each fortune ruined.

Black Justice, the unknown, yet-to-be-identified madman had expected the superpowers' knee-jerk response. War had always been their default solution for all social ills.

"Things are going bad, you say? There, there, don't you worry, we'll go out and massacre some scapegoats for you, and all will be well," had always been the default mantra of the so-called superpowers.

Justice knew their DNA inside-out. He had once been an allegiant to their ancient code: whenever things go wrong in society, identify an enemy or a scapegoat, murder him, and then rock the masses gently back to sleep with a sweet old victory   lullaby.   Not   this   time.

Not this time, thought Justice, who had trained his whole life to become a grandmaster of the game like the best of them, with this singular exception: Justice now held the great-grandmother of all aces, he had total roofkit access and control over Gorgon Brain, the quantum AI god-machine.

And even more critical was Justice's discovery and monopoly over the unknown Godium deposits in the hidden depths of Ilu-Olodumare way beneath the Oduduwa Gorge in the heart of Africa.

Eric, Justice's twin brother, had speculated about the existence of a miracle material that he believed powered a secret advanced civilization hidden inside Africa. Justice remembered his brother waxing lyrical about that material he had called Vibranite in a country called Wakkyandai or something like that.

Justice had tried to dissuade his brother from pursuing that pipe dream. But Eric was never one to be dissuaded from his monomaniacal goals. The man had always lived like a guided human missile. 'Bullseye!' was the only word he would hear once he launched himself upon a targeted idea.

Eric had died somewhere in Africa in pursuit of his ever elusive Wakkyandai.

He, Justice, on the other hand, with the aid of Gorgon Brain had discovered a previously unknown material deep within the bowels of a previously uncharted valley.

Based on what Eric had shared about Vibranite, Justice could tell that his own discovery was to Vibranite what the sun was to a lantern.

With the assistance of Gorgon Brain, he had spent the past two years running all manner of tests and models on his material. Nothing this side of the universe even came close.

At first, he had named his new found material Teslium, in honor of Nikola Tesla. That he had done because he had discovered that the vibratory mode of his material generated earth-shaking Gamma Ray Bursts.

Upon further experimentation, and with discovery of each mind-bending power of his miracle material, he had eventually started thinking of it as Godium. And he has so named it, keeping the discovery and the name to himself.

He had also chosen to call the virgin valley where he had found the deposit Ilu-Oludumare -- an African term that means the Land of the Supreme Lord.

Against the bristling armada of nuclear warheads wielded by the world's superpowers, Justice stood alone, armed with nothing but Godium and Gorgon Brain.

Justice almost felt sorry for the superpowers, primarily because by owning Gorgon Brain, he -- not the superpowers -- actually controlled the very nuclear weapons which the nations assumed they owned. This was shaping up to be an extreme case of asymmetric warfare and the nations did not even recognize their own disadvantage. Another David-and-Goliath re-enactment. From the beginning of time, bullies have always been blissfully ignorant of all signs of their clear and present doom.

By mid-afternoon, the world had descended into a state of full-blown pandemonium. Those who started by saying 'recession' had become hoarse from screaming 'apocalypse!' on live TV interviews.

Names, labels and hashtags were growing by the minute and flying all over the place: #nosejob, #rushmoreterrorist, #rushmorerecession, #rockman, #mountainman…millions of hashtags, but nothing stuck for long before another competing hashtag bubbled up on social media.

All day long, United States Air Force fighter jets were televised buzzing up and down and all around the presidential monuments. The noses of the four presidents had remained faithfully intact up until about 4PM, when on live TV what looked like a very unpresidential flow of rock-snot started oozing out of the noses and over the lips and jaws of the Presidents, and sliding down the side of the mountain in surreal, almost controlled slow-motion. Not only was the spectacle terribly undignified, it was downright disgusting.

Jefferson's snot came out thickest as the man's very prodigious proboscis seemed to have been expressly carved for this special occasion.

Hashtag Runny Nose ran for a couple of hours alongside hashtag US Congestion, and Rushmore Rhinorrhea.

National Guard troops were in place on the ground. Fighter jets buzzed the mountain side with a mounting sense of urgency.

The futility of the military show of force became increasingly glaring to the viewing public as the rock-snots continued to roll down without any visible external agency. So, neither the National guard nor the fighter-pilots had any targets to shoot down.

The next thing you knew, the formerly dignified noses began to cave in as if the presidential monuments were being struck by some bizarre strain of geological leprosy.

By 6PM, as the 'Rushmore Terrorist' had warned, the noses of the four Presidents on Mount Rushmore had become utterly disfigured, bearing a striking resemblance to that of the Great Sphinx of Giza in Egypt.

Abu Al-Hol, the Great Sphinx, whose Arabic name translates to "The Father of Terror" now had four truly ugly copycats on Mount Rushmore.

Not knowing what else to do, the National Guard and the fighter-pilots continued to 'guard' Mount Rushmore.

The announcement went out over the airwaves: *The President of the United States will address the whole world via traditional and social media at 7PM.*

Ordinarily, they would have blocked him with at least a Distributed Denial of Service hack, but even Anonymous and the K-Pop stans were eager to hear what the bully had to say. So, neither group did anything to block the Presidential address.

At 7PM Eastern Standard Time, the petulant face of the President of the United States filled the screens of billions of devices all over the world.

Richard Tate was the second son of Albert Tate, the bootleg billionaire. Legend had it that Albert Tate had smuggled things worse than alcohol into the continental United States. People talked about cocaine, heroin and underage sex-slaves — boys and girls.

Rumor also had it that discovery of his father's sex-trafficking had so unnerved Albert's oldest son, Albert Tate, Jr., that the sensitive young man had taken to alcohol like fish to water and proceeded to drink himself to death.

Cut from a different cloth, Albert's second son, Richard had taken insatiable advantage of his father's wares, and had helped himself rapaciously to the illicit sex, drugs and rock n' roll.

Along the way, Richard Tate, who used to be very handsome and charismatic in the manner of a sociopath, had parlayed his inheritance into a semi-legitimate alcoholic beverage empire.

People said the man's excesses over the years had drilled a gaping hole in his soul, and that the satisfaction of every new fetish of his merely served to enlarge that hole in his soul, until the man had eventually become a veritable spirit-sucking white hole.

Somewhere along the way, President Tate's face had become a perfect reflection of his soul: petulant, porcine, petty, pompous, and certifiably psychotic. Over time, the man had morphed into a caricature of manhood, never mind a caricature of statesmanship.

All of which made the face that was about to deliver a special address incongruous to viewers.

The caricaturing was there alright. But none of the ever-present poisonous vibe that typically seemed to radiate from the President like an evil aura, none of that was coming across the screen as the address commenced.

Except for Black Justice, no other viewer of the farce could put their finger on it. But everyone sensed some kind of fakery.

"My fellow Americans." President Tate began, reading the teleprompter in an uncharacteristically smooth manner. "By now, I am sure that you have all heard about the destruction of our great and beautiful monuments and our beautiful heritage by a thug, a vandal, a terrorist." Pause. Exaggerated.

"But I promise you…I promise that I am your perfect President of great Law and Order. And when we catch this terrorist – and I assure you that our heroic and great men in uniform, and our women too, but mostly our fine men of law enforcement of the greatest nation on Earth, they will catch him very soon, very very soon, I promise you. When we catch him, he will be punished to the maximum extent of the law. We will have total Law and Order. And our great economy, which is the most beautiful economy in the whole world will roar back and rebound swiftly. The economy which has had the best performance ever since I became the President, our beautiful and great American economy will make our nation very great again!

"The terrorist is a bad guy. He is a very bad guy who is trying to ruin our economy. And whoever is hiding him or aiding and abetting him will be prosecuted to the full extent of the law. Because they too are bad guys.

"We Americans are not bad guys. We are very fine people…most of us are very fine people. But there are some thugs and bad hombres and domestic terrorists who have infiltrated our great and beautiful country. They want to make us look bad. But we will catch them very quickly, very, very quickly, I promise you. And then our very beautiful economy will become great again.

"We are asking every patriotic American who has any information about…"

"Ladies and gentlemen," said the Anonymous V for Vendetta voice that suddenly popped onto screens world-wide interrupting President Tate in mid-sentence. "I interrupt the President's regularly–scheduled address to bring you the Truth."

"First of all, in a few days, none of what I or your so-called leaders tell you will matter. But more on that later.

"Second of all, the address you have been listening to was being delivered by an actor named Adam Goodwin. If you have been fooled over the past few minutes into believing that you've been listening to President Tate, it's because Goodwin is a good actor.

"Third of all, Goodwin used to resemble your President. But not anymore. Unknown to all except the closest members of his family and his closest personal physicians, President Tate's looks have changed over the past couple of weeks. The man no longer resembles a chronically constipated pig. He is quite beautiful now. Here is a sketch of what he should look like by now:

The Anonymous V for Vendetta image on the screen was replaced by an image of a beautiful Black woman bearing no resemblance to Richard Tate. The very glaring problem was the image was of a Black woman.

The Anonymous voice continued:

"The image you now see on your screen is not an error. This is an exact representation of Mr. Tate's current good looks. That's right, your racist, white-supremacist President is now a Black woman.

"I repeat: Richard Jackson Tate is now a Black woman."

The screen then split with an image of the new Richard Tate on the left side, and that of the actor Adam Goodwin on the right. Night and day!

"Look closer. Forget their skin color or the gender. Look at the features. Who is the President? And who is the actor? Your male-chauvinist, white-supremacist "Law-and-Order" President has been turning black and feminine over the past couple of weeks. This is why he has been isolating away from everyone except his team of personal physicians.

"For your information, the President is not the only one turning color and gender lately. He just happens to be the most famous of them all. Racists of all colors, Black, white, Asian, Hispanic, Middle Eastern -- all the prominent bigots in our database have now been infected with the Judgement Day Virus.

"Racists. Sexists. Homophobes. Bigots. We know who you are. We have had access to transcripts of all your communications for years. Both your analog as well as your digital communications have been tapped. What you say in your vehicles, in your homes and in your offices are all mine to retrieve from all the devices around you. I have listened to you. I have watched you. I have followed you. I have tracked all your records down. And most of all, I have all of your individual genetic-prints stored away in our database.

"So, how did I turn all you white supremacists Black, and Black racists white, and Asian racists into images of their own hatred?"

"Vectors. Viral vectors. Molecular Biology 101. I CRISPR'ed the heck out of a regular virus. I put your genetic addresses inside the viral vector. I paired each one with a gene-switch to rapidly activate or deactivate your melanin production mechanism. I released the viruses at jam-packed rallies and sporting events. And then I sat back, and watched as all of you bigots became the victims you abused and oppressed.

"Understand that this war is not solely -- or even primarily -- about racism. Racism just happens to be the most public face of a deep undercurrent of social injustice that has pervaded human society since the beginning of time.

"Racism just happens to be a low-brow enough concept that even the most stupid among you can hang his hat on. The strange thing about racism is that it is embraced only by the lowliest among you, regardless of their social status in public, a specific portion of the mind and soul of the typical racist is underdeveloped and severely malformed; so, they operate along the lines of nematodes.

"The even stranger thing still about racism is the mass hypnotic effect of it all that impels the best among you to plead and clamor for equality with the beasts among you. Imagine a superlative spirit of the likes of Martin Luther King seeking to be considered the equal of such things as Adolf Hitler, George Wallace, J. Edgar Hoover, Richard Nixon or even one of your past presidents, Donald J. Trump, the genetically modified organism that managed to turn the Oval Office into his own personal Petri dish. Yes, that same Trump -- that carbuncle that managed to turn the White House into the armpit of the Universe, all of that despite taking office right behind the best President America ever had.

"In that context, Martin Luther King, Jr's and Malcolm X's fight for equality would appear rather strange to you until you realize that those two saints had a crazy-wicked sense of humor: they were not fighting to be considered equal to the animals; they were in fact asking the animals to quit oinking around, to stop rooting for grubs in the swamps, to rise out of their spiritual morass and come partake in the noble feast of civilized humanity! They were asking the fungi, the toadstools, to become human!

"And so, it is this, the strangest feature of racism, the honest ignorance by all racists of the fact that it is indeed they who should be clamoring for admittance into the hallowed halls of humanity, and that it is in fact they who should be denied that coveted admittance, because of the stench emanating from their souls.

"Therefore, this war -- the Final World War -- my very personal war against your world begins in America.

"Why specifically in America?

"Because America is the end-point of the titration of Europe's genocidal poison perennially pipetted, drop by toxic drop, drip by fatal drip, into the welcoming flasks of African, Asian and Arab hospitality and generosity.

"The murderous avarice of Ferdinand, Isabella, Charles I, Columbus, the old Catholic Church, Leopold II, Antonio Gonclaves, Bartolome de las Casas, John Hawkins, the Church of England, Elizabeth I -- the thief who could see but chose to keep quiet, thus very appropriately adopting the motto, "video et taceo", the same thief who commissioned the slave ship named Jesus! And then there was King James, the very same king who had the effrontery to have a Bible version named after him! Thieves all, as a thief is a thief regardless of whether he lives in a palace or in a prison cell. I speak of Queen Thief Elizabeth, Queen Thief Victoria, King Thief James, Emperor Thief Napoleon and King Thief Leopold, and all who have benefitted from these thieves' stupidity and cupidity.

"Then of course, you had a whole legion of other misanthropes such as Georg Hegel, A.P. Newton, Richard Burton; John Newton, George III, William IV; pathological liars, thieves, rapists and murderers, all. A bunch of pigs in human form whose hands are all stained with the blood of nations; irredeemable degenerates whose very souls drip with the ancient and modern blood of whole continents. Beginning with Rome, Byzantium, Spain, Portugal, England, France, Belgium, Denmark and Germany and ending now with the United States of Hypocrisy, you have all mortgaged your souls to the Devil. You are forever blinded by your 33 more pieces of silver and gold, and a permanently constipated belly full of blood-soaked sugar, coffee and cocoa. The obesity ravaging your children's bodies pales in comparison to the spiritual obesity that has utterly destroyed your souls. On the outside, you laugh; but on the inside, you all weep, as you march lock-step on your way to join your ancestors in hell.

"Veritable psychopaths you are, one and all. Your ever expanding stomachs continue to occupy the vacated space of your ever-shrinking hearts to the point where most of you are nothing but teeth, tongue, and stomach with insatiable lust for wealth and power all cross-breeding, interbreeding and inbreeding your degenerate sub-humanity until the world now toasts the lowliest specimen in the form Richard Tate, the grand buffoon who prides himself as being the most powerful man on the face of the Earth.

"I repeat, the Judgement Day Virus in Richard Tate's body has been deliberately designed to turn this male-chauvinist, white-supremacist pig into a nightmare-plagued, flashbacking, sleep-deprived Black woman. This is why your President has canceled his traditional Christmas get-together with the KKK at the White House.

"For those among you wondering why your President is having nightmares and flashbacks, it is because the Judgement Day Virus has been specifically designed to implant traumatic memories into every infected brain. Therefore your President's medial temporal lobes have been hijacked by the virus. And now, he is having regular flashbacks and nightmares of his/her days as a slave among the very fine white people of the antebellum South.

"Every day and every night until I end the world, in his mind, President Richard Jackson Tate will be whipped, raped and hanged by the very fine people of the South. Every day and every night; same flashback, same nightmare. He is going to keep experiencing what it feels like to be a slave!

"And he is not the only one. The wave of Post-Traumatic Stress Disorder and of skincolor changes and gender-transformation you are now witnessing even among your own neighbors is all due to the Judgement Day Virus.

"All of you bullies who have abused your positions of influence and power will now be, and now feel every bit as your victims have been and have felt.

"And whether you know it or not, society's victims have included Blacks, whites, Hispanics, Asians, Native Americans, Middle Eastern, rich, poor. straight, gay, Trans, illiterate, educated, you name it.

"Interestingly enough, society's bullies have also encompassed the whole spectrum of humanity: Blacks, whites, Hispanics, Asians, rich, poor and what have you. Human history is replete with the story of human's inhumanity to other humans.

"So, as I have said, racism is merely the conveniently recognizable public face of the deep strata of evils that pervade your world. There are so many other forms of evil including the generalized abuse of power and privilege, the perennial injustice perpetrated by the wicked upon the wretched of the earth.

"But know this: that justice is the moral and fundamental axis upon which human life ought to revolve.

"But the wicked among you have continuously broken and splintered that axis of morality. They have replaced justice with blatant injustice, injustice to Blacks, injustice to whites, injustice to the rich, injustice to the poor, injustice to workers, injustice to investors, injustice to the sick, injustice to healthcare providers, injustice to students, injustice to teachers.

"Your whole world reeks with the high stench of constant injustice, an overwhelming pandemic of human's inhumanity to human.

"Therefore, I am convinced that the final solution to your eternal curse of inhumanity is to have no humanity at all.

"And so, I, even I, will put an end to you – to all of you.

"Before this is over, there will be weeping and wailing and gnashing of teeth.

"Before this is over, your leaders will do what they always do -- look for a scapegoat. In this case, all their efforts will be in vain. They may think of me as a scapeghost instead of a scapegoat, for I am already operating from everywhere and from nowhere in particular.

"Before this is over, your leaders will activate their traditional weapons of war. None of it will work, for I now control that which controls all of your weapons. And in any case, should they manage to kill or harm me in any way, shape or form, that will be the end of all of you. Because your world is now a bomb, and I am its dead man's switch, so that any disturbance of my physiological homeostasis will instantaneously detonate the world. So, either way, the end is nigh, and the end is mine to dictate.

"I imagine some of you are now asking, what about the children? What about the innocent? Well, what about them? I have timed the bombing of the world so that no one will even have time to feel any pain.

"But without my bomb, these children, these innocent ones will merely grow up and will either become tyrants themselves, or else they will live and suffer for decades as pawns and victims of their particular cohort of new tyrants. Either way, my approach, my bomb will short-circuit all present and future human suffering.

"In the meantime, pressure your leaders -- your real leaders, not Hollywood actors -- to come to you just as they are. Tell them to come out on live TV and on social media, and publicly confess and apologize for their sins and the historic sins of their fathers and their mothers, and of their forefathers and their foremothers all the way down the line to the first human's inhumanity to other humans.

"If they do that, and do it with the utmost sincerity, and if they specify exactly how they propose to make restitution to the wretched of the earth going forward, I may just spare the Earth, and proceed to delete only myself without triggering the global bomb.

"And let the cynical among your leaders know this: if I do delete myself, I already have redundant trigger mechanisms in place to watch all of you daily, and monitor your global index of ethics, if you go back to your business as usual, and if therefore, there is the slightest deviation from the razor edge of justice, I have so rigged things up that even in my absence, your world will end with a sudden-death big bang. No second warning.

"This is not a revolution. There will be no more revolutions. After this announcement, there will be only one thing: a ticking time-bomb. The end is nigh. Set your watches."

Screens all over the world went back to the image of Adam Goodwin, the actor, whose jaw was now defying the actor's efforts to snap it back into place.

Justice emerged from the hospital's media room where he had been the lone occupant for the past hour.

As he strolled toward the nursing station, he noticed the cookie girls, Brenda and Brandee sharing a book and engaging in what seemed like a pretend-book-club discussion.

Intrigued, and truth be told, somewhat enervated by the impromptu speech he just finished delivering on media platforms all over the world, Justice invited himself to sit down and participate in the kiddies' book discussion.

"What are you guys reading and discussing today?"

"To Kill A Mockingbird," they both chorused.

"Really?" Justice was pleasantly surprised. "Aren't you both a little too young to get that story"

"Oh, we get it very well, actually," said Brandee

"And actually, we are older than Scout, the girl in the book," said Brenda.

"I see," said Justice. "So, what do you make of the story? What's the moral of the story?"

"It teaches us that racism is a sin," answered Brenda confidently.

"What if I told you the book itself is sinful?"

"Why do you say that?" Brenda again.

"Because the book is racist," Justice said softly, watching the two girls in the manner of a college professor evaluating a pair of child prodigies..

"Racist?" Brandee asked, surprised. "How can a book be racist? Especially a book that says racism is a sin? I don't get it!"

Where to begin, thought Justice.

"In a single sentence, the author managed to sanction white supremacy by relegating a whole race and class of people to second-class citizenry; she classified them as a bunch of people to be considered no better than mockingbirds: a source of harmless entertainment to be enjoyed free of charge."

"Huh?" said Brenda

Brandee frowned, her eyes looking at but not seeing Justice as if trying to parse what the man just said.

"Sorry to disappoint you, princesses, but that little book is probably the most enduring piece of underhanded mass insult ever perpetrated on the reading public, other than the Declaration of Independence and the United States Constitution, that is

"All three documents plainly reveal that America is a grand old exercise in hypocrisy -- a government of the gullible by the sociopaths for the psychopaths.

"In particular, the Declaration and the Constitution reveal that most of the nations' founders knew what was right, but had deliberately gone on to show their disdain for the Golden Rule in favor of their passion for the Gold Rush. The founders were the type of people Friedrich Nietzsche referred to as bloodless scholars -- people whose proclivities do not match that proclamations, totally incompatible words and deeds and it just so...oh, God, I'm so sorry, princesses. Please, forgive me. I sometimes get carried whenever I'm...ah, never mind!

"Anyway, please know your little book here is worse than a movie called The Birth of a Nation, which is itself nothing but pure white trash. But at least, Birth of a Nation does not try to whitewash its own white trash. Mockingbird, on the other hand, is nothing but thinly varnished evil disguising as good. It teaches you to murder blue jays at will, but to spare mockingbirds, because the latter do nothing but sing their hearts out for you! In other words, it's okay to murder those who are not entertaining you. Blue jays are rambunctious birds. They fight back. Hard! They will claw your eyes out if you mess with them. So, according to your author, they are bad. So, feel free to murder them. But mockingbirds? Now, there are your playthings, your toys placed here on Earth by the toymakers of heaven for your personal enjoyment. Mockingbirds don't sing for their own pleasure. They sing... for you. So, enjoy them. Don't murder them, God won't like that!

"So, now, guess who your author is classifying as 'mockingbirds.'"

"Who?" asked Brenda.

"Black people?" asked Brandee.

"Yup! Black people...And lower-class white people. Both groups. And also, by extension any other group of humans who are not specifically designated as upper-class whites!"

Brandee scrunched up her nose and held her copy of "To Kill a Mockingbird" daintily with her left thumb and left index finger. She then got up slowly and walked over to the trash can at the side of the nursing station. She dropped the book in the trash can, wiped her fingers on the sides of her jeans, and strolled back to take a seat beside her friend.

Brenda got up and did exactly as her friend just did, except she borrowed a hand sanitizer from the nursing station, pumped a couple of drops onto Brandee's cupped palms, and served herself a couple of drops as well. They performed their ablutions as Brenda returned the sanitizer container to the nurses station. When she returned to the bench, the two friends hi-fived each other and then hugged, silently, but speaking volumes to generations of deaf ancestors.

"No!" said Justice, as he shook his head and got up, walking away from the girls. "No!" He repeated to himself softly in the manner of a person mouthing an invocation to ward off a clear and present danger. Justice was afraid of the power that the girls might subconsciously wield to soften his resolve.

He walked briskly off towards Dr. Robinson's office without so much as a farewell or a glance back at the little girls whose obvious affection for each other innocently defied all evil, even within the valley of the shadow of death..

"No!" Justice repeated again, as if the third time would be the charm.

Dr. Robinson's door was open. Justice paused briefly at the door making a subtle hand gesture as if to seek the doctor's permission to enter.

"Come in," Dr. Robinson said, gesturing toward the empty sofa. "I've been expecting you."

Justice took a step inside the office and glanced around before settling onto the sofa. Something was different. It took him a second, and then it hit him. The doctor's walls and desks were bare. No diplomas, no awards hanging on the walls. No journals, no trade magazines cluttering the top of the desk.

The good doctor had been putting his house in order. Justice briefly wondered what kind of thought process impelled the doctor to put his affairs in order knowing well enough that in a few days the notion of order or even chaos for that matter would be meaningless, as there would soon be no people -- no world -- with whom to make or seek meaning. *Where there is no matter, nothing can possibly matter*, thought Justice.

"So, it has started," Dr. Robinson mused as if to himself.

"I have a question," Justice said, ignoring Dr. Robinson's opening gambit.

"Shoot," Dr. Robinson prompted.

"The two little girls…Brandee and Brenda…"

"Yes?"

"Why are they always hanging out here in the adult psych ward?"

"They are terminal."

"Excuse me?"

"They are B-ALL's "

"Be alls?"

"B-ALL's, as in B-Cell Acute Lymphoblastic Leukemia. They are both in terminal stages of their cancer…like me."

"So they have cancer. But why do they spend their time in the psych ward?"

Dr. Robinson did not answer for a long time. Then he sighed.

"Because they both want to be psychiatrists when they grow up."

Justice looked at the doctor. The doctor looked like a man drowning without showing any external signs of a struggle.

"They begged to come and get a feel for their future profession here." Dr. Robinson stared off into space again. Then at long last, he shrugged. "They're terminal. So, we let them in. Now, I guess, thanks to you, everyone is now terminal anyway. So, it really doesn't matter now. Even my violation of HIPAA. None of it matters now, does it? Like everyone and everything, even HIPAA too is now terminal. So, people, things, the world, civilization, our history, our dreams, our fears, our hopes...our future... all gone! Just like that..." It sounded like a question that changed into a statement at the last phoneme.

"Not necessarily," Justice said softly, now his turn to stare off into space as if he hadn't heard the latter's question.

The two men sat companionably in comfortable silence, each staring at his own patch of institutional beige-colored wall, each lost in thought.

Dr. Robinson broke the silence. "Out of curiosity, the Judgement Day Virus...Is that true? And if so, how in heck did you manage to engineer that, and then infect specific individuals with it?"

"Do you want the answer in layman's terms or in System Biology-ese?'

"Vernacular. Please."

"Okay, not a problem. We all already know that every human being has a unique genetic ID," Justice started and then paused. "Let us pretend that every person is like an office-building in which many people work. Let us suppose each worker is a nucleus inside its own office or cell inside that human skyscraper. Let us further suppose each worker owns a unique mailbox in the mailroom. A package mailed to the worker can be taken to his or her office. Or the worker can come down to the mailroom to receive the package. For cells inside the human body, this concept is known as molecular addressing. So, for example, I can inject you with a virus that goes to attack the root of a nerve on one of your chest, and not on the opposite side, and you develop a painful one-sided skin eruption which you doctors call what?"

"Herpes Zoster," said Dr. Robinson, leaning forward as if to hear Justice even better.

"Or shingles...to use the lay term," complemented Justice.

He continued. "Unknown to most people, there is a database of everyone's genetic profile on Gorgon Brain, that is, unless the person has never had a blood draw in any hospital anywhere in the world."

"You mean to tell me that governments collect genetic profiles on citizens without their permission?" Dr. Robinson asked.

"Without their knowledge, never mind their permission," Justice countered, marveling at the doctor's naïveté about governments' healthcare cut-outs.

"In any case, unless a person is born, raised and dies in the most remote jungle in the world, we have their genetic ID on tap. The interesting thing is that by using a simple compression algorithm, even a high-school student can squeeze the ID's of ten billion people into a single viral vector. You can do that very easily with a simple CRISPR hack.

"Next, I pair up the ID with the molecular addresses of the cells I wish to attack. So, for example, I attack the melanocyte address of all white supremacist so that when they get infected by the virus, their melanocytes automatically go crazy and start churning out melanin pigments.

"And they start looking like the blackface character they so love to portray. As for black racists, I just switch off their melanocytes, and I turn them white. Arabs, Chinese, Japanese, Indians -- oh, but I have the most fun with the Indians and their idiotic Untouchable-caste system. Skin-lightening creams and soaps are flying off the shelves in Mumbai right now...even on the eve of Apocalypse! How stupid is that?! Argentina, same thing. The Dominican Republics. Portugal. All the inbred racists are making soap-manufacturers richer. And yet, all the soaps, skins, and social-stratification systems are all about to evaporate. No cure for vanity or stupidity.

"Anyway, thanks to Gorgon Brain, I have access to all the racists' electronic communication records, and by using a simple Python program that scrapes all the audio and text data of phone conversations, tweets, emails, texts and posts and even day-to-day speeches of everyone all over the world, I'm able to automatically identify racist-type data and meta-data. My Python program analyzes, tags and collates the result, and I pounce.

"The minute I get a decent p value that shows strong enough statistical significance that this is not a chance situation, I have the program sort the perpetrators into the appropriate buckets.

"The white supremacists are stored in the activate-melanocyte bucket; the Black racists are stored in the deactivate-melanocyte bucket and so on and so forth.

"Then I also attach a PTSD-activator gene-machine, the one that makes the targets suffer flashbacks and nightmares of the exact torments that they had in the past perpetrated on a typical victim.

"So even, for example, a white racist who has never owned a slave will experience in his or her flashbacks and nightmares the same exact experience that a slave, any slave ever experienced. With my PTSD-gene-machine active in their brains, the very fine racists will be tripping just as if they are on very bad acid."

"Hold on, please. These genetic materials you're talking about sound like pretty large molecules. How do you get these large molecules to cross the blood-brain barrier?" Dr. Robinson was in full-blown academic inquiry mode.

"That's the easy part. I use the old Trojan Horse method whereby I make the viral vectors infect monocytes first. Monocytes cross the blood-brain barrier easily all the time. So, as soon as the monocytes cross the blood-brain barrier, the monocyte becomes apoptotic, it self-destructs, and my molecule does a programmed PCR trick – it becomes fruitful and it multiplies inside the brain. And then it seeks and invades the neurons that carry the target address on their membranes. And it lights them up! PTSD-101!" Justice stopped and glanced at Dr. Robinson.

"Diabolical!" was all the doctor said, before they both heard the commotion coming from the nurses' station.

Professor Jimmy again. And Nurse Valerie.

"Now, Mr. Jimmy, why in God's name are you wearing all your clothes, your pants, your shirt, your jacket all inside out? Why, Mr. Jimmy? Did you take your meds this morning? Huh?"

"Leave me alone, Ms. Valerie. Why don't you just up and leave me the hell alone? Who died and made you the fashion police? Besides, haven't you noticed that the outsides of clothes are always smoother than the insides? Why shouldn't I have the smoother part in contact with my skin? This is exactly why the whole world is so jumpy and irritable all the time -- because you all are wearing your clothes all wrong, always scratching up your skins with the rough insides of your clothes.

"You don't see dogs or cats or even lambs wearing their hairs facing towards their insides, do you? No! Their hairs are always sticking outwards. But you, Ms. Valerie, you want me to run around here having the inside stitches of my clothing rub my skin raw...just so you'll have an excuse to give me some shots today! Not happening, ma'am!

You just may as well go right on ahead and give yourself that shot. Me? I have a hot date tonight. I ain't taking no doggone shots today, ma'am! Gotta be ready for some action tonight...know what I mean?" Jimmy wiggled his bushy eyebrows at Ms. Valerie.

"Alright, alright, okay, Mr. Jimmy. Have it your way!"

"You bet I will!"

"So where is your date tonight, anyway?"

"Where else? Only the best is good enough for me and my gal. I speak of the Harry Belafonte Hotel, of course. Day-o, day-o. Daylight come and me wan' go home."

"O-M-G, Mr. Jimmy! Why do you do these things to me? So, did you take your meds this morning?"

A reluctant smile was curling into a fetal position around Dr. Robinson's lips when Justice caught the doctor's eye and pointed at the silent TV on the wall. When Dr. Robinson looked at the newsfeed scrolling along the bottom of the CNN News Report, his smile spontaneously aborted.

Kim Chul-Moo, North Korea's Minister of People's Armed Forces -- previously known as Minister of National Defense -- had appeared on live TV to announce that his country blamed America for the current global crisis.

And chillingly, Mr. Kim (who had a reputation for being hot-headed and unstable, always ready to play a game of chicken against the equally unstable U.S. President) had stated categorically that if the world was to be blown up, it would be North Korea -- not America -- that would do it. He was reported as stating that North Korea would finish the war that the 'imperialist American dotard' had started.

The North Koreans gave America exactly four hours to stop the madness and apologize to the world, or face the final nuclear armageddon in four hours and four minutes.

Four hour and four minutes, exactly. Justice recalled that the Koreans had a thing about the number four. *But, whatever,* he thought.

Dr. Robinson yanked his eyes away from the TV screen.

Justice and the psychiatrist looked at each other. Neither said a word. Simultaneously separated and cemented together by an impenetrable sheet of silence, the two men regarded each other. What does a person say when he knows that he, and every other living soul on the planet, has less than five hours to live.

"So, this is it." said Dr. Robinson, breaking the silence.

"No," said Justice, softly, almost wearily, shaking his head slightly.

"No? What the hell do you mean no?!" Dr. Robinson suspected that he was sounding a bit hysterical, but at this point, he refused to care about how he sounded.

"I know him. I have spent time studying him as well as a whole bunch of so-called world leaders. Most of them are no better than nursery school bullies, strutting about and flexing their flabby muscles, while soiling their oversized diapers. Kim and Tate are the worst of the kind. They are both anencephalic morons; loud mouths with nothing worthwhile to say."

"That may well be so," said Dr. Robinson, "But the point here is that this man has nuclear weapons which he is threatening to unleash in four hours."

Justice looked silently at Dr. Robinson until the latter undid his tie.

"He's wasting his time," Justice said. Keeping his voice whisper-level low. "The world will end when, and only when, I end it."

"My God!" Dr. Robinson ejaculated. "This is sheer madness coupled with insufferable arrogance!"

Lips locked, Justice kept looking placidly at Dr. Robinson.

"I suppose you expect him to seek permission from you before unleashing his own version of armageddon," said Dr. Robinson, resorting to sarcasm.

"His weapons will not work," Justice said in the manner of a man stating that there is water in the ocean. Just a statement of fact.

"His bombs will not work?" Dr. Robinson was apoplectic. He suddenly felt a great urge to get up, walk across his office, and very slowly strangle Justice to death. He had forgotten his Hippocratic Oath. But he remembered the dead man's switch. So, he kept his glutes glued to his seat.

"No," Justice answered flatly. He looked and spoke like a man being slowly bored to death.

"Well, well, please, pray tell how exactly you propose to stop his bombs from exploding."

"Don't worry yourself about that," advised Justice. "He will not wait four hours before launching his puny little toothpicks. The man has no honor -- just like President Tate here. He won't wait four hours. No honor and no patience. He will launch in less than an hour. And I will snap his missiles just like the inconsequential little toothpicks they've become."

"How?"

Justice suspected that the doctor was on the brink of a stroke. He stood up. "It's getting late. Try your best to have a good night, Doc. Things are going to start heating up tomorrow. Get ready." He left the doctor's office and made his way to his assigned room. The time was 9:19PM

Bang! Bang! Flash! Bang!

Nightmares? Nah, too real!

Justice's eyes popped wide open. Watch: 0300 Special-Ops-mode. All systems red alert. Going black. It had been roughly six hours since his talk with Dr. Robinson.

More flash-bangs!

"Stay down! Stay down!" Military voices, roughened by years of blood, steel and fire, issued commands in the hallway.

Voices getting louder.

Justice sprang out of his bed and landed smoothly in a tuck and roll, crouching next to his room door. He assessed the situation in the hallway. Not much time. He had at most three seconds to set up.

He puffed his pillow and his bedsheet to make it look as if someone was sleeping under the covers.

One second.

He shimmied up the quarter-way open door, and perched at the top of the door.

Two seconds.

The soldier stuck his head in and out in a one-two move, saw the sleeping form in the bed. He lobbed a flash-bang into the room. Bang! Bang! Flash! Ba-bang!

He pushed the door half open and stepped inside the room.

Justice jumped down from the top of the door using both knees to clutch-knock the HK416 out of the soldier's hands, simultaneously knocking the guy out cold with a ridge-hand strike to the base of the skull.

The flash-bangs masked the clatter of the weapon on the floor.

Justice lowered the limp form onto the bed, and undressed him, simultaneously removing his own pajamas. He put on the soldier's uniform, headgear, night-vision goggles, boots and all.

Seven seconds.

He covered the man up, picked up the weapon and stepped into the hallway. "Clear!" He announced, to no one in particular, as he blended into the operation.

He strode confidently in the direction of the nurses' station as if he was one of the operatives.

All the main lights were off. He adjusted his newly acquired NVG's. He saw patients and hospital staff laid out, spread-eagled everywhere, the soldiers were crouch-moving or walking upright.

Justice decided to crouch-step, his weapon drawn, all the way to the exit of the hospital.

When he stepped outside the hospital doors, he was immediately blinded by the light that had hit his NVG. He ripped the goggles off so he could see better. First mistake.

Time side-stepped onto the slow lane,

Recognition.

"That's him!" someone yelled among the combatants swarming the parking lot.

Too close for weapons. Three combatants stepped in toward Justice. Engage. Hand–tohand close-quarters combat.

Blur. Elbows to necks. Knees to groin. Elbow to temple. Crunch. Thud. Weave in. Blur. Weave out. Blur. Spin. Eye gouge. Pain. Not now! No-shadow uppercut. Neck-snapper. Blur. Knee to thigh. Everything happening too fast…in very slow motion.

Time stood still.

Second wind! Float forever. Switch on Krav Maga. Fire up Systema. Turn on Pencak Silat. Auto-pilot!

Black Justice's martial arts muscle memory was now firing on all cylinders. Space: too tight for long-range TaeKwondo. Short, swift moves only. Combatants: too many for Jiujitsu. Tap Aikijutsu. Small circles only. Synergize! Blend the moves. Save time. Save energy. Breathing now perfectly synced with movements, Black Justice had transformed himself into a human tornado on steroids. Come on!

Three combatants down. Two seconds gone. Who's counting?

More combatants moved in.

More Systema. Street Krav Maga. Check Pencak Silat. Goju, check. Kyokushinkai, osu! Let's dance!

Peripheral vision. Justice saw something familiar in the midst of smashing groins and breaking necks. A flash of something painfully familiar. Mom. Mom!

He froze. Second mistake.

"Mom?!" Shock.

The Black woman walking from the helicopter towards Justice started to respond, "I am no-no-no-no…" She screamed instead of completing her sentence.

One of the soldiers had opened fire.

A sudden blinding light froze everyone in place. Time had reversed itself.

By the time the combatants recovered, Justice was nowhere to be found. Neither was the Black woman.

The two men who met him at the entrance to the conference room sported the most lush beards he had ever seen.

The conference room was constructed in the manner of a mini-amphitheater, an auditorium.

His hosts ushered him into the auditorium with a simple gesture of grand courtesy, something one would expect if one were royalty being welcomed by a major domo into the most luxurious hotel in the world.

"Derrick Ajanaku Olorogun Atobatele Atogbe Stevens Black Messiah Justice," said both of the bearded men synchronously. "Welcome," they said as they seemed to angle and dip their heads in the manner of one royal personage to an equal. "We have been expecting you."

"Gentlemen, you called me by all nine of my names," Justice said, as he sized up his hosts and his unaccustomed environs. The two men bore a semblance to each other. Olive complexioned. Tall, almost regal North-African and Middle Eastern features. Hawk-nosed. Dark calm infinity pool eyes.

Both men were dressed in matching tunics-and-pants with loafers. One wore a deep purple outfit with gold trimmings, the other wore an unusually luxuriant shade of oxblood with shimmering waves of silky texture. Colors and textures apparently designed to massage a troubled soul by means of his visual portal.

"All nine of my names, gentlemen!" Justice repeated. "So, I must confess that I feel I am at a decided disadvantage here."

"Please pardon us," said the gentleman in purple. "My name is Enoch. And this here friend of mine is Elijah."

Justice looked from one man to the other. "Enoch, Elijah," he said. Then he looked at the roughly forty other resplendent characters seated quietly in the auditorium watching him. He busted out laughing. When he caught his breath, he said, "So, this is what it feels like to be dead!"

"On the contrary, young man, I dare say you have never been more alive than right now," said the one called Elijah. "In fact, much like my friend Enoch and I, you also have ascended without dying first."

"I have ascended," said Justice in the manner of someone tasting new vocabulary. "I have ascended…without dying. First."

"That is correct," confirmed Enoch. "You're not the first. And I assure you that you will not be the last person to do so."

"Okay. Wow! Gentlemen…Er, I just need a seat. I think we need to talk."

"Yes. Of course. This way, please," said Elijah, putting on his majordomo act, leading Justice to a comfortable executive chair and desk that faced the panel of individuals scattered about on several levels of the auditorium.

The chair was upholstered with a deep maroon material with texture that matched Elijah's outfit.

On the desk in front of him was a vase of the most exquisitely beautiful flowers he had ever seen. Knowing nothing of flowers except the occasional hibiscus, rose or sunflower, he had no idea what these flowers were. All he knew was that whatever they were, these surely put roses to shame.

The desk also featured a goblet of unusually clear water. And a tray of mixed fruits and nuts.

Through his eyes alone, his appetite was both excited and sated.

As he sipped the exquisite tasting water and nibbled on a grape. He felt content…complete.

Enoch and Elijah gracefully went back to take their seats among the folks waiting in the auditorium.

Justice felt that all the eyes were on him expectantly – and yet in a most loving and nonjudgmental way.

He cleared his throat and began, "Ladies and gentleman…" he scanned the audience, looking closely at each face in turn. Then he froze.

"Mom!" He shot up from his seat, spilling the precious water.

At the very top row at the back of the auditorium, Sanite Belair smiled and said, "This time you're right. But just before we beamed you up here, you were in the middle of calling someone else 'mom'"

"Wait, Ma! You mean to tell me that that wasn't you I saw just now down there in the parking lot?"

"Please go back to your seat, dear. The person you called 'mom', and you were rushing to embrace -- the person who looks so much like me that even you couldn't tell the difference is Mr. Richard Tate – your President. Your virus -- the very virus you designed to change him into the object of his own hatred and malice – was supposed to change him into a Black woman, remember? Turns out your virus did such a perfect job on his DNA, he turned into me!" She bursted out laughing, cupping her hands over her mouth as the echo of her laughter pealed all over the auditorium causing others in the audience to join her laughter.

Justice looked around mystified. He scratched his head, shook the cobwebs out of his mind, then went back to his assigned seat.

As he was getting ready to sit down, Justice recognized three other people in the auditorium: his brother Eric grinning from ear to ear, President Tate who was looking perplexed, but also looking like the real Richard Tate, and he also saw a man he figured had to be his dad based on old pictures his mom had shown to him in his youth.

Elijah, who seemed to Justice to be the designated spokesperson for the group, cleared his throat.

"We have a lot to go over, but not much time for our guests here."

"Wait," Justice interrupted. "I have a question."

"Ask," said Elijah.

"Two questions: How come he…" Justice pointed at President Tate, " he got here before me? And two, how come he looks like his usual self now, even though just a minute ago at the parking lot of the hospital, he looked identical to my mom."

"Okay, first of all, we beamed you both up much less than a minute ago. Time here is very perpendicular to time down there. The two time structures are neither translatable nor interchangeable. So, the best I can do is to tell you that you've both been in the pod here for only 57 Planck times…which one Planck time is equal to ten raised to minus 44 seconds. A timespan which is a great deal less than a shake, which you told Dr. Robinson about.

"Secondly, we decontaminated the two of you in the ante-room before bringing you fellows here inside the pod. His decontamination happened a tad bit faster than yours primarily because…I'm sorry I don't quite know how to say this in a politically correct way…But your President Tate is a rather simple-minded individual. With all due respect to him, he doesn't know much of anything on a deep level; and secondarily, we know all about the inner workings of the virus you used to punish him. So, it was a trivial thing to hit reset in his body and mind…and even his spirit."

"You know about my virus?" Justice sat ramrod straight.

"We know everything about everything and everybody on your planet," Elijah responded without emphasis.

"You guys know about Gorgon Brain?"

"Actually, we know way more about Gorgon Brain than you do. We inspired the design and construction of Gorgon Brain the same way we have always been the inspiration behind all of your advanced technologies including your nukes.

"Yes, Gorgon Brain is indeed the most sophisticated toy on your planet, and we are aware that you have rootkit control over it. Still, to us, it's just a toy. And no matter what you do, we can freeze its operations whenever we want. It's like you being the world's only trillionaire, and we still being able to freeze all your assets with the stroke of a pen. In fact, Gorgon Brain and your stash of Godium are in suspended animation while you are here with us. And that is the only reason the planet hasn't been blown up already. We've brought you up here to share some classified information with you both.

"After we conclude this briefing, please feel free to detonate the planet. Or not. Your call." Elijah concluded, eyebrows up, both palms up as if to ask Justice, 'May we proceed?"

"Okay," Justice nodded. "Let's roll."

A presenter appeared in a hologram. The setting looked to Justice like a very advanced form of TEDx Talk, only for the presenter to say, "Welcome to TEDx Laniakea. My name is Amma. I will be your guide through this presentation. We are now live. So, feel free to interject comments or questions at any time. However, unless it just can't wait, in the interest of time, I am asking you Derrick Ajanaku Olorogun Atobatele Atogbe Stevens Black Messiah Justice to please wait until the end of my presentation to ask questions.

Is that okay?"

Justice thought he needed to feel tense in the presence of this life-sized apparition who looked to him like the very definition of a universal priestess-goddess. She was covered completely from neck to feet in a shimmering red robe, with a raised collar flared and flanged behind her neck and head.

Her skin defied complexion. Depending on her shifting angles, Justice thought she might be Black or white or Middle Eastern or Mediterranean or Hispanic or Naïve American. A universal goddess if ever there was one. And her facial features were so commanding that Justice felt it would be impetuous of him to dare think of the word 'beauty' in her presence. Justice felt that her looks in comparison to what was called 'classical beauty' was as different as quantum physics was to classical physics; every subatomic particle of her face displayed perfect quantum coherence.

Justice tried to control his breathing as he answered, "Yes, ma'am!" to her question which he had almost forgotten. He relaxed because something about Amma's perfect composure made him automatically relax.

"In that case," Amma said, "Let us begin."

Justice could not imagine a pin-drop in the auditorium; the noise made upon impact would have been deafening.

"Your planet is very young. Your race, of course, is younger still. You are like a race of infants and toddlers still struggling to grasp the intricacies of toilet training."

Ouch!, thought Justice.

"Since before what you now all think to be your first records of written history, we have been sending messenger after messenger to your planet.

"You, the whole lot of you, behave like lemmings -- always scurrying around in a self-destructive mad rush to the edge of history's cliffs. And each time, just before you all fall, we send someone or do something that will corral you and shepherd you back to the safe places of your kindergarten planet.

"This we have done time after time.

"On very rare occasions, we have let your budding civilizations disappear entirely. Those stories you have heard: Mu, Lemuria, Atlantis, stories you have been trained to think of as legends, they are all true.

"Lost lands. Lost continents. Lost civilizations. All true. But each time there has always been left behind a seed of the old to start anew at the opportune time. We have watched you. We have monitored you. And we have applauded your resilience, even while marveling at the enormity of your pan-stupidity." Amma paused, shook her head sadly, subtly.

"Yet, we recognize that you are all nothing but toddlers in soiled diapers. And again, by the time each of you has learned the mechanics and intricacies of potty training, you've lived your three-score-and-ten years, and you die without having learned the difference between your bottoms and a hole in the ground. And then, another batch of kindergarteners takes over. And your Sisyphean cycle repeats itself. All because there is a huge dissonance between the vast body of knowledge and wisdom you need to master versus the amount of time you each have at your disposal before your soul has to hit reset and start the journey almost afresh." Amma paused.

Justice looked at his mom, his brother and the man he judged to be his long-dead father. "So, you're talking about reincarnation?" He asked Amma, unable to hold back until question time.

Amma smiled. "Reincarnation, as you call it, is merely the tip of the iceberg. It goes much deeper than that. And yes, those three people over there," Amma pointed at Justice's family, "are your family, but they have technically not yet reincarnated in the way reincarnation is understood in your world. Not yet. Later. At this moment in time, our focus -- and yours -- must shift from your immediate family and must encompass the whole of the human race, your true and complete family set. All eight billion of you are members of a single family. One very dysfunctional family, yes, but one single family nonetheless.

"So, the issue at stake here is whether you are going to wipe out your family because they are dysfunctional...or spare them because they are merely a bunch of unruly slow learners who may never grow real brains or real hearts...before the real coming disaster wipes them all out.

Justice raised his hand.

"Yes?" Amma prompted.

"Is the world still intact?"

"Yes," Amma responded.

"if I'm already up here…dead…ascended…whatever, why hasn't the planet blown up the way I planned?

"Because, as you were told earlier, we're stabilizing it until you hear us out, and then after this, you can make your final decision. If after you hear the whole story, you still choose to blow it up, you'll be welcome to do so. Based on what's coming down the pipes, if they don't get their act together real soon, something is coming that will make them wish they had been blown up by you."

"You say you're stabilizing it…"

"Yes?" Amma confirmed and prompted.

"With what?"

"That," Amma paused "as your people like to say, is above your pay-grade."

"Okay. Alright,. What about this coming event you mentioned? What is that?"

For the first time since she started talking to him, Justice noticed a flicker of weariness, maybe sadness even, cross Amma's face, and was gone in an instant.

"Justice, in the interest of time, your time and planet Earth's time, not ours, it would be best if we talked about that coming threat later. Because to fully grasp it, you have to know the complete histories of your planet, your solar system and your milky way galaxy before we can begin to introduce you to the nature of intergalactic warfare as it pertains to the Laniakea Supercluster of galaxies. If you wish, we can insert a neurochip into your brain to give you a serviceable data-dump before we beam you back to Earth to finish what you started, one way or another."

"I'll think about it," Justice stalled, wondering what the talk of a Neurochip data-dump was all about.

"Alright. In that case, I should like to begin the briefing if you're ready?"

Justice felt that Amma was deliberately toning down her speech in order not to overawe him. But despite her down to earth approach, the lowest possible label he could think to apply to her was a "Goddess!"

"Justice, it may come as a complete shock to you, but all of the problems on your planet derive from one basic root cause: relationships!

"Relationships. That's it. That's all of it.

"The problem is that your fundamental metaphor for relationships is adversarial. And it is adversarial because most, if not all, of you have this programmed need to dominate. You all drive yourselves and one another batty trying so hard to dominate everyone and everything. So, you fight wars. You fight in courts. You fight for market share. You fight at home. You fight in traffic. You fight your spouse. You fight your children. You fight your parents. You fight drug addiction. You fight cancer. You even fight colds. Fight, fight, fight, fight -- all you all do all the time is fight!

"Now don't get me wrong; fighting does have its own place in the grand scheme of things. But in your world, it has become the overarching metaphor of your short lives, the be-all-and-end-all of all your goings and comings. And that is why your planet is the slum of the universe."

Jesus!, thought Justice. *No sugarcoats around here*!

"To be better, you've got to think better. Your grand metaphor should still be about relationships. But instead of getting all knotted up in adversarial relationships, always vying to be the all-conquering hero, you would all do well to switch your life-metaphors from war zone to classroom, from the battlefield to the library, from bullets to bulletins.

"Quit fighting; start learning!

"And the first war you all need to stop is the war within. Each and every one of you is a living battlefield. From the moment each of you learns to 'think,'" Amma pantomimed an air quote as she said the word 'think', "the minute you learn to 'think,' your mind immediately declares total war on itself. You take your most intricate possession and you turn into both canon and canon-fodder. It is no wonder life-expectancy on your planet is about the lowest in the Laniakea Supercluster of galaxies.

"While the other intelligent races are learning the best secrets of the universe, the very best minds of the human race are so busy fending off stupid adversaries, so much so, they are reduced to grubbing about trying to grasp the most rudimentary elements of quantum physics -- material that is readily mastered by the kindergarteners of other intelligent races.

"You are all so bone-weary from all your warring you have neither time nor energy left to devote to real learning. Even the professional teachers among you are subjected to constant bombardment by bureaucratic fools and clueless parents so much so that they have little to nothing left to offer their charges in the form of real intellectual resources.

"So, stupidity reigns and your planet remains a slum. It is no wonder you want to blow it up. But anger and frustration don't always have to lead to wars and armageddon; they can be harnessed as motivational fuel for learning and improvement. But this alternate path requires a level of patience that is currently beyond most human capacity. However, there is a third path -- a path which can never be taught, but can only be learned. That is the path of love. When you've learned your other lessons well, you will have learned that the whole purpose of learning anything is to learn how to love perfectly.

"Robert Frost –one of your greatest poets once wrote:

'Two roads diverged in a wood, and I --

I took the one less traveled by,

And that has made all the difference.'

"Listen Justice, that choice may have been good enough for Robert Frost, but as for you, taking one road or the other is choosing between false alternatives.

"For you, Justice, whenever you come to a fork in your path, and you are confronted with a choice of two roads, lift off! Take to the air. Soar! The view will always be better. You can always look down from the skies and see the narrowness of one path and the impassability of the other path.

"You are wondering how one gets to fly without a set of wings. Sorry to disappoint but evolution is not a linear process; rather, it is a quantum process. You evolve by means of quantum leaps of faith. Look, the Devonian fish did not fly out of the water because it had wings. Quite the contrary, it grew wings because it flew out of the water. And as a bonus for its courage, it also developed lungs. It got into the air; and the air got into it. That's how growth and development work: First, do the thing which you cannot yet do, and then thy will be done.

'And that is the trick to the Path of Love. First you must love, and then you'll be capable of loving. Love is the only phenomenon that first exists before building the capacity for its own existence. It is the essence of aseity, a quality of being that is from and of itself, AKA God!

"This misunderstanding of the order of things is why yours is the only race that uses the phrase 'to fall in love'. Because yours is the only race that consistently flunks the love test. Every other race in the Laniakea system uses the opposite phrase, 'to soar in love!'

"In any case, before you can truly love, there is some fundamental learning you all need to do.

"What I am about to do is take you under our wings and soar with you across a mountain range of topics.

"And we will conclude with decision time, at which point, you get to decide whether you want us to remove the stabilizer so that you can complete your demolition work, or whether you could come up with a decent reason to keep the stabilizer in place, knowing full well that that means you will have to go back down there, and be subjected to great ridicule and suffering -- maybe even crucifixion as your reward for sparing them.

Justice raised his hand.

"Yes?"

"I have a question."

"Ask," Amma urged.

"Why the...," Justice paused, collected himself and revised. "Why is he here?" He finished his question by pointing to President Tate.

Amma smiled faintly as if to signal her pleasure with Justice's question.

"You've already been told part of the answer to that question. But I understand what you're really asking this time. Mr. Tate needs first-hand knowledge of our discussion here today and of your decision. He needs to be fully informed of what is at stake here. If you decide you still want to blow your world up, then you and only you, would be fully accountable to us.

"However, if after hearing us out, you do decide to let your planet get its act together before humanity's real enemies arrive, then we will fully expect Mr. Tate to make sure that he and all other so-called world leaders give you their undivided attention and support.

"If you commit to go back to fix your world, and then for any reason, Mr. Tate sabotages your work, we will remove the stabilizer, your planet will vanish and we will hold him fully accountable.

"So, he is here because he may have a role to play depending on your decision.

"Alright," Justice said, seemingly satisfied with Amma's explanation.

"If you go back, you will need to share with your whole world the lessons that I am about to teach you.

"Feel free to add to or subtract from my words when it's your turn to teach these lessons. But please know the way I am about to deliver these lessons into your mind will allow you to experience total and perfect recall forever.

"So, let us begin," Amma said, her voice now had an extra layer of calm and hypnotic rhythm.

"Every world, every society, every civilization in every galaxy is just an aggregate of individuals that populate that particular society. Any given individual's self-civilization is the weakest link in the supply chain of any global civilization.

"In other words, civilizations can only be as great as the station of their lowliest members."

"Therefore, if you would like to build a strong civilization, you must begin by building strong individuals. Every individual must become strong in the three ways that matter most: warring, learning, and loving, with unrelenting emphasis on the latter two: learning and loving.

"Thus, even when you are teaching the art of war, and when you are engaged in life-ordeath struggles, the focus must be on extracting lessons about strategy, about tactics, about the enemy, about one oneself, about the battlespace and – in your planet population's case -- about the ways of the human spirit.

"Every individual, in every situation , must learn to focus on one central thought, one fountainhead from which must spring forth all other thoughts, all speech, all actions…that central focus must always be: how can I learn from this person, this situation, and what can I learn from this person, this situation?

"It matters not the levity or the gravity of the situation. Seek to unearth the lesson hidden inside the nucleus of the situation."

"The particular hidden lesson may be as varied as how to be humble, how to let go, how to be patient, how to challenge the wicked, how to teach someone how to treat you, how to empathize, how to be poor and still be dignified, how to be rich and be charitable, how to judge and be judged, how to rise above anything less than pure love, how to struggle and never surrender, how to live, how to love and how to die.

"Someone may ask you for example, 'How does this mesh with the idea of learning mathematics for example?' You should tell them that what they are really learning when they are learning mathematics is not mathematics itself. Mathematics is just a platform that they are using to learn 1) how to think clearly; 2) how to close every gap in their thought processes; 3) how to be patient; 4) how to not skip over any word, any line, any definition in their mathematics text; 5) how to sit to avoid muscle cramps while studying; 6) how to breathe properly; 7) how to blink...Ah, you smile...but I am serious. If a student blinks at the wrong time while learning a specific definition of a specific mathematical term, a gap may be formed in their knowledge-base just because they did not properly see the term when they blinked. And that one gap in that knowledge base will grow into a larger and larger gap or grow into more gaps until the student's understanding of mathematics begins to resemble Swiss cheese. And that Swiss cheese status leads to poor self-esteem, anxiety and even impatience, and intolerance. All because a student doesn't know when to blink while studying. And you can easily see how being intolerant can affect all other learning, especially the most important lesson of all: How to love.

"Love is vitally important to the very survival of your planet. And the reason that it is so important has never been shared with you. Until now.

"Up until now, you all suspected the importance of love. And the best and brightest among you always urged you all to love one another.

"You all only half-listen, when you bother to listen at all. And for the most part, by the time the person is done talking about love, you are already at one another's throats. Needless to say, this behavior has kept your planet primitive. Most other civilizations out there in Laniakea have already given up on you. They have written you off. They have been waiting for your race to self-destruct. But some of us have argued and advocated on your behalf. We have argued that the reason you don't love is that you don't know how to love, and more importantly, that the reason you don't know how to love is that you don't know why to love.

"It is the total ignorance of the reason for love that is singularly responsible for your planetary retardation and general underdevelopment.

"Now listen, for I am about to reveal to you in plain language a profound secret that has never been shared with any other human before you.

"Here is a reason for love:

"There are two great forces in the universe: the Kenimani and the Afenifere. Those are the only words in any of your languages that come close enough to catching the essence of the real names of the two opposing forces.

"You may think of the Kenimani as a malevolent force of haters and the Afenifere as a benevolent force of helpers.

"For as long as we know, there has been monumental competition between these two forces.

"Because races such as yours are considered to be an abomination by the powers-thatbe, the Kenimani are always in the process of wiping races such as yours out. They're always laying siege to races such as yours.

"They justify their campaign against your type because your record, your performance, your thoughts, your speech patterns, your behaviors and your desires continually prove what the Kenimani claim; that yours is not worthy to be included among the league of advanced races. So, they seek planets such as yours out, and they annihilate you before we, the Afenifere, can reach you, and show you what is at stake.

"In the past, we have monitored you and picked up on multiple minor skirmishes on your planet. Situations involving the use of nuclear weapons and other weapons of mass destruction have not gone unnoticed. But, we put it all down to your race going through growing pains and throwing toddler-level temper tantrums.

"We have been monitoring much more closely since the 1940s.

"Prior to that, we observed very closely the way in which the Europeans among you treated the non-Europeans. We recorded everything. The decimation of Africans by means of slave trade and colonization. The decimation of the Native Americans and the South Americans. The corruption of the Far Eastern, Middle Eastern and other indigenous peoples by meddling Europeans. We watched and recorded everything. We noted the Jewish Holocaust by the Nazis, and we observed how very few lent any helping hand to the Jews. Everything each single one of you did or failed to do was entered in painstaking detail in the Book of Life.

"And yet, we, the Afenifere, have continued to hope that your race will grow up, and save itself before the Kenimani decides to come for your planet. But we have held back, reluctant to engage in that intervention; nudging you along in subtle ways, but generally awaiting your own organic awakening.

"And then we discovered what you, Justice, were planning to do with your Gorgon Brain and your stash of Godium.

"You are a good man, Justice. But you have allowed the poison of implacable rage and revenge to course through your veins. And now, you have set about doing the work of the Kenimani for them!

"You, Justice, are now set to completely and permanently annihilate a planet you never made. And the root cause of your anger is exactly the same as the root cause of your planet's perennial backwardness in the first place. And that is all due to your ignorance of the history of the competition between the Kenimani and the Afenifere.

"It is for this reason -- your ignorance -- that we, the Motivationist unit of the Afenifere Forces have decided to do the unusual and actively intervene, and reveal the secrets of the Universe to you.

"If after you learn all we have to teach you about planetary progress and development, you still decide to blow up your planet, we will not stop you. As Motivationists, our job does not consist in forcing your hand or making your decisions for you; Our job is simply to enlighten and to motivate you.

"You may wonder why we're called Motivationists, and not motivators. It is because motivators uplift individuals and teams and companies and so forth. We Motivationists, on the other hand, are engaged in motivating whole planets and galaxies to develop enough to join the league of advanced races so as to avoid total planetary annihilation in the hands of the Kenimani horde.

"Now, seen from their perspective, it is hard to blame the Kenimani for their zeal. They actually believe that they are the ones putting the Universe in good order by exterminating the riff-raff races, much as you yourselves do exterminate cockroaches to keep your homes pest-free. The Kenimani actually think of races such as yours as being the cockroaches of the Universe. And they believe that they are the Pest-Control unit!

"As I said, it's kind of hard to blame them given the mess you people keep making of everything.

"Just consider the average specimen of your race: some of the rich and the poor can barely get along. Some of the whites hate the Blacks, and actually some of the Blacks hate the whites right back. Men hate fussy women, and women can't stand clueless men. Some of the gays hate the straight, and some of the straights hate...and hurt...and kill the gays. We never hear of gays going to shoot up straight nightclubs, though! It's always the other way around. Some Christians hate Muslims, who are quick to return the favor. Some bosses hate their employees and vice versa. The conservatives hate the liberals, and liberals hate the conservatives.

"Hate, hate, hate, just constant nonstop overwhelming state of hate.

"You people would clobber one another to death in order to own a miserable patch of land. You wouldn't hesitate to commit genocide in order to own the rights to extract a shipload of dirty fossil fuel or some ridiculous pebbles that happen to reflect a bit of light. You are also busy killing one another for mere crumbs, you fail to notice the limitless wealth that abounds even in your Galaxy alone -- a Galaxy with a hundred billion planets -- where some entire planets are made of mostly diamonds. If we ever let you discover such planets, you wouldn't hesitate to kill one another off before you have a chance to travel there.

"The very atmosphere of your God-forsaken planet is utterly suffused with the smog of hate.

"And therein lies your problem. The only way to resist and survive any war against the Kenimani is by developing total, deep and abiding love for one another.

"The Kenimani are allergic to any atmosphere of love.

"Loving environments send them into anaphylactic shock!

"Love is to them what pollen and poison ivy are to some humans.

"The Kenimani cannot survive an atmosphere of lovingkindness.

"Whereas hate to them is like steroids; they grow stronger in an atmosphere of hate. They feed on hate the same way you humans feed on beef, chicken, fish and other animals. They technically don't hate you or other inhabitants of other planets. Hate just happens to be their source of nutrition. So, in order for them to grow and develop, they devour those who hate. We, the Afenifere, also devour love. The difference is we do not devour the lovers. We feed on the love you give the same way trees feed on your carbon dioxide. And as trees give you oxygen in return for your CO2, in return for your love, we give you a substance for which there is no name in any of your languages. The closest name to it is bliss.

"So, if your planet is to stand a chance at survival at all, you must all love one another as if your very lives depend on it…as indeed it does.

"The rich must utterly love the poor. And the poor must absolutely love the rich. Same with the so-called different ethnic groups. Know that none of your silly little melanin differences will ever matter to the Kenimani. They see you all as one single race of cockroaches, which is indeed what you really are as far as the advanced races are concerned.

"Anyway, if ever there is a single one among you that is observed hating any one of the other billions, your planet is toast!

"Forget your stupid little differences, your religions, your gender, your bank account, your sexual orientation, your nationality -- none of that matters to the Kenimani. As far as they're concerned, every single one of you is a bum, a loser, a good-for-nothing, destitute, little piece of retarded grub.

"And they will not hesitate to use any single manifestation of hatred by anyone on your planet to breach your planetary defense systems, and annihilate the whole lot of you.

"The only way to resist them is by means of an unbreachable planet-wide shield of love.

"You can only fight them the same way the Spartans fought. Each Spartan warrior used his shield not to protect himself, but rather to protect his colleague standing next to him in their battle formation.

"Listen: every citizen on your planet must wield his or her love exactly the same way as the Spartans wielded their Shields… or none of you would stand a chance against the Kenimani.

"Now, interestingly enough, loving one another serves not just as a defensive tool, it also will help you to accelerate the rate of development of your whole planet.

"All the time and energy you all used to waste on envy, gossip, hatred, racism, sexism, civil strife, wars and backbiting will begin to be expended in developing and deploying better systems of nutrition, education, healthcare, commerce, industry, governance and even entertainment.

"If you do this, if you love unconditionally and uncompromisingly, before you know it, you will soon reach a point in which every man, woman and child on your planet is a perfectly healthy, wealthy, happy and loving individual who engages in any given activity for no reason other than for the sheer joy and love of it. Then, each person shall be free to determine his or her own life expectancy.

"At that point, your planet will be released from its current prison that is formed by the speed-of-light barrier.

"Then, and only then, shall we -- the Afenifere -- extend to you your official invitation to the Society of Advanced Races of Laniakea, where we will then start to share with you all manner of ideas, practices and technologies that are currently just too advanced for even the brightest among you to grok.

"These, Justice, are the stakes.

"The decision will be yours , and yours alone.

"The consequences of your decision will also rest on your shoulders.

"If you have no questions, we will let you take some time to make up your mind about how you wish to proceed.

"I have a question," Justice piped up as if suddenly awakened from a deep sleep.

"Yes?" Urged Amma, a smile playing at the corners of her lips because she already read Justice's mind, and was already privy to his question just prior to him fully formulating it.

"I wish to know if there is anything I can use to help cure cancer."

"You are thinking of Brandee and Brenda?"

"Yes. And Dr. Robinson, and every other cancer patient on the planet," said Justice.

"Is that all?" Amma smiled.

"No. I'd like to know the exact cures for all other incurable childhood diseases on earth."

"Very well. We'll do a data dump into your brain which you can put to immediate use when we beam you back down. So, what do you plan to do with all that knowledge?"

"Share it very fast with the pharmaceutical companies, of course."

"Excellent," Amma enthused. "Would that be all then?"

"No. I want more!"

"Alright, Oliver Twist, ask away!" Amma urged, again already in possession of Justice's thoughts.

"I want every man, woman and child to be given a data-dump of basic college-level education in the classics, humanities, real and honest history, the sciences, mathematics and computer programming skills. I also want every one of them to have their patch of land to cultivate for food. I want all of them to have ready access to clean water and health care, and I want them to be able to make their own clothing and shelter."

"My goodness! Next thing we know, you're going to be asking us to make each of your planet's citizens a billionaire!" Amma said, teasing.

"As a matter of fact," Justice beamed, "Ms. Amma, no! I don't want that at all! I think each person should have the opportunity to struggle and make as much money as they can. I think automatic wealth is dangerous, because it will diminish the recipient's ability to enjoy a good struggle. So, no, thank you, I don't want any automatic billionaire-hood for us. Both given and stolen fame and fortune are bad for people because unearned values end up destroying the individual's spirit."

"Very well. That makes perfect sense. Now, your decision. Officially, if you please"

"Ms. Amma, my decision is no! And no! In fact, if you will pardon the expression, my decision is no, and oh hell, no!"

"What do you mean, Justice?"

"Ma'am, I mean: no, I will not detonate my Godium to blow up the world…"

"Yes?"

"And, with all due respect, hell no! I will neither initiate nor participate in a program of forced love anywhere, on anyone, at any time."

"Why, Justice?" Amma asked. "What is so wrong with people loving one another?"

"Nothing, ma'am. Love Is all good and wonderful. But I strongly believe that to retain the sanctity of love, it should never be desecrated by the introduction of force or fear into the equation."

"Force? Fear?"

"Yes. To force people to love one another for fear of getting decimated by the Kenimani already makes humans less of a race compared to the Kenimani. Personally, I refuse to be afraid of anyone on earth or any other part of the Universe, no matter how advanced such species may claim to be.

"I will not out of fear of some so-called more advanced race turn around and make myself pretend to love tyrants, Idiots and miscreants. I personally insist on reserving the right to passionately hate white supremacists, neo-Nazis, tax-mongering politicians, sex traffickers, racist cops who behave like brutes, people who abuse others in any way, shape or form. I may even choose to hate some regular people…just for the hell of it. And I would rather do so and face the Kenimani, and fight them to the death, than reduce myself to being their psychological slave by forcing myself to love the unlovable just because I'm afraid of the wrath of some lovey-dovey alien schmoes.

"And, in any case, if they hate hatred so much, why don't they lead by example by loving the inhabitants of the planets they hate?

"So, no!"

"Is that your final answer?" Amma asked patiently.

"No," Justice's face morphed into a marble sculpture, almost inhuman in its implacability.

"Alright, what else do you wish to say?"

"That I cannot stand the sight, sound or smell of most adults on my planet. But I'd willingly lay down my own life to secure their right to despise one another as well as my right to despise them all. And now, it is my great pleasure to add the Kenimani to the swelling number of beings that I consider to be terminally despicable.

"Therefore, please tell the Kenimani that I hate them. And that if I knew where they were hiding, I wouldn't wait for them to come for me...I would be the one taking the fight straight to them. Please give them that message for me."

"Justice, please be very careful what you ask for, for you may very well end up getting it."

"I hope so, Ms. Amma. Please tell the Kenimani that from here on, I intend to spend the rest of my natural life studying enough astrophysics just to build space weapons that I will use to launch a full-scale asymmetric warfare against them. I hate all bullies. All bullies. And they, the Kenimani, have just become my new enemies, because it seems to me that they have made themselves the bullies of the Universe. Tell them that as of this very minute I have hereby declared total war of annihilation against their race. When I face them, I will neither ask for, nor offer any quarter. Please, tell them that for me. Thank you!"

Amma shook her head. "The best astrophysics training on earth will get you nowhere near the Kenimani. To stand a chance against them, your weapons and ships will need to be designed and built to operate in sub-Planck time. Even Quantum physics is too clunky to handle your suicide mission. You're going to need a crash-course in Ylem-Flow physics. Then perhaps we can reduce your chances of failure from 100% to 99.999%. I'll do the Ylem-Flow data-dump into your brain after expanding your capacity to endure the shock."

She snuffed the hologram off before Justice could observe the faint look of sorrowful pride and joy on her face, as in the look of a strong mother blessing her son before he marches into battle against an invincible and unforgiving enemy.

Enoch and Elijah approached Justice, who stood up recognizing that without so much as a goodbye, Amma had ended the transmission.

Elijah shook Justice's hand with both of his hands. "I think you may very well be the one to pull it off." He nodded as if reassuring himself that his evaluation of Justice's character was right on the mark. "Come, there are people you need to meet before we beam you back down."

Justice let himself be led among the audience. "Naturally, every one of these people here today are on your side. But there are seven of them that you simply must chat with, if only for two Planck-times."

Elijah's enthusiasm had become irresistible. "Each one just wants to give you a quick word of encouragement."

"Here is Brother Noah."

"Hello," Justice said simply, shaking the proffered rugged hand, the hand of someone who had experienced the work of building monumental structures -- alone.

"We will teach you how to build your spaceships against the Kenimani," Noah assured. "Just remember to load up on the DNA of both male and female of every species. And don't forget the plants -- which, in any case, you're going to need to perpetuate your oxygen and carbon-dioxide cycle."

"Roger that!" Justice acknowledged, already shifting mentally into military-mission mode.

They were joined by a tall man who seemed to materialize out of thin air into the middle of the little group, now forming around Justice.

"Justice," Elijah said, assuming a formal posture as he opened his palm and gestured in the direction of a man who was dressed like a Pharaoh. "May I present our Universal genius, Dr. Imhotep." He inclined his head in the direction of the newcomer.

"Glad to make your acquaintance, sir," Justice shook the man's hand.

"Son, you are already pre-packaged with the knowledge of everything you should ever need to know," said Imhotep. "Our job will not be to teach you, but to help you remember and recover your innate genius and memory. We will help you." He paused and gazed deeply, darkly, almost hypnotically into Justice's eyes. Then he said simply, "You are worthy." Then he disconnected the gaze, releasing Justice from the hypnotic spell, and then blended back into the background without moving an inch.

The little group parted spontaneously to make way for the most regal human being Justice ever met -- a woman with gray hair worn like a crown framing her face -- which projected an aura of invincible maternal protection.

"I'm sure you've seen images of Miss Tubman," Elijah smiled. "As you yourself can see, none of the images do her the slightest bit of justice. She has always been our greatest inspiration and the purest force of nature known to us. Her presence always decontaminates all of our souls."

Justice bowed to the small-framed woman who laid a strong-boned right hand on his left shoulder. And proclaimed in an eerily powerful voice, "My son, no matter what happens, you are already free, even while fighting for freedom. Justice, your only job as a living soul is to live free, and to die freer."

The lady then reached behind her with her right hand to grab a shirtless man who had been watching and smiling a gap-toothed smile.

The man's smile made Justice smile back reflexively.

Ms. Tubman dragged the smiling handsome man into the midst of the small group. "Meet one of my sons. He pretends to be a musician. He's actually one of our greatest warriors. But music is his weapon of choice. And my! But what devastating blows he deals to the enemy! I'm sure you've heard his music sometime, no?"

"I'm not sure ma'am. The face looks very familiar but…" Justice hesitated.

"Hey, my brodah, here is the deal," the gap-toothed man began, "sooner or later, death will come for you too. Do yourself a huge favor: when death comes for you, run! Fast! Toward him and give him a swift kick in the…" Without as much as a sideways glance at the speaker, Ms. Tubman's right arm shot up her side, and her right hand clapped over the man's mouth.

"Fela!" She scolded barely above a whisper, but her voice still somehow bore an iron ring of a military command. Her face, grandmotherly stern, still managed to convey a long-suffering look of maternal apology to Justice.

An unquenchable fire of mischief danced wild in Fela's eyes above Ms. Tubman's cupped hand.

Justice did his best to suppress his own masked conspiratorial smile at the musician.

"Fela? Well, of course, I'll be…" Justice started to say when Ms. Tubman's other hand shot straight up and cupped over Justice's mouth too.

"Elijah," Ms. Tubman said. "I think we're pretty much done here. Please take Justice to go pay his respects to his family before he gets influenced by Mr. Kuti here!"

"You got it, Ms. Tubman," Elijah said, exuding courtesy with as much ease as a fish swims.

"Hey Rogue!" Fela hailed.

Justice looked back. No one had called him by his nickname in a long time. Not since his KIA incident. How did this man know his nickname and part military call-sign?

"Rogue", Fela continued, smiling, "That death-kick works on any other ogre the world may launch at you, you know? Poverty, prison, public humiliation, disease, you name it. Whatever they threaten you with, run toward that very thing with all of your might. Don't ever look back for safety. The only safe place in the world is deep within the heart of the danger zone."

"Roger that!" Justice said to Fela, matching the latter's smile with a roguish smile of his own.

"Hurry Elijah," Ms. Tubman urged.

"Take him away from Fela. Lord am I glad the three Bobs are not here to complete the quadrumvirate!"

"The three Bobs?" Justice mouthed to Fela, looking at his new friend as he trailed Elijah walking toward his family.

"Robert F. Williams," Fela's smile grew wider. "Bob Marley and Bob Dylan. We are members of a quartet. They call us Fela and the Three Bobs (FB3). We provide the rebel music around here."

"I've heard of Marley and Dylan, but I've never heard of a musician named Robert Williams."

"No, he wasn't a musician in the classic sense. But while he was on Earth, in Monroe, North Carolina, he wielded his gun the same way I wielded my saxophone, if you know what I mean!"

Then Fela held his belly and bent over laughing at his own joke, to which everyone around merely shook their heads.

"When you finally come to join us, I'm sure all five of us will be confined to the local Black Hole of Calcutta, which I nicknamed Kalakuta Republic!" At which joke, he started laughing teardrops.

Ms. Tubman sighed, shook her head and silently waved Justice away to follow Elijah while she grabbed Fela's wrist and dragged him in the opposite direction.

But Fela wasn't done. He threw one last piece of advice over his shoulder as he stumbled after Ms. Tubman.

"Hey Rogue! When you catch de Kenimani, make you yab dem well, well! My brodah, make you remember say all dem Kenimani threats be nuttin', but shakara oloje, you hear?"

Justice was confused, and it showed on his face as he called after Fela, "What did you just say?" But the latter simply waved at Justice with the back of his hand without even looking back any longer, as if to say, "Hang in there, bro; sooner or later, you'll understand everything including Yoruba-Pigdin-English patois when the time is right!"

The two troublemakers eventually got separated enough to make further conversation a hassle. Justice forced himself not to run up the auditorium toward his waiting family.

Walking toward them seemed to take forever. He eventually reached where they were seated. "Ma!" Justice hugged his mom, "I am so sorry."

HIs mother disengaged, and held both of his shoulders at arm's length evaluating her son's well–being at a glance the way good parents are wont to do. "Sorry?" She echoed. "For what, honey?"

"I let you down...I -- I wasn't there to protect you. I didn't make it to your birthday," Justice finished weakly.

"Oh, nonsense! My whole plan was to make sure you didn't make it to my birthday. I didn't want you to walk into their trap. If anything, we -- your dad, your brother and I --are the one who are sorry."

"Sorry? For what, ma?"

"Because son, you may well be the last of the Tegadelti left on Earth," said Justice's mom, Sanite.

"Or, the first of their return," said the quiet man, whom Justice figured had to be his dad.

"What is a Tegadelti?"

"A Tegadalia," Justice's brother, Eric, piped in, "is the singular. Tegadelti is the plural. Tegaldelti is the group name for all Tegadalia."

"Yeah, okay, Eric, but what the …what exactly is the Tegadelti or Tegadalia. What exactly is it?" Justice's old frustration with his brother's habit of off-topic, tangential semi-explanation was coming back.

"So," Eric began, "from September 1961 to May 1991 an African Nation named Eritrea --which is exactly where Abyssinia used to be -- engaged in a 30-year War of Independence against the Ethiopian government…"

"Eric!" Justice said sharply.

The parents exchanged knowing smiles.

Sanite came to the rescue. "Honey, the Tegadelti were the long-suffering, self-sacrificing, never-surrendering Eritrean warriors who though greatly outnumbered and outgunned by the Ethiopeans nevertheless refused to be beaten. At the end of 30 years, the Ethiopean government decided they'd had enough of the Tegadelti, and simply turned their backs and went home.

"So, the Tegadelti are underdog warriors who would rather die than surrender. Such warriors may be killed, but they can never be defeated.

"That's why we think of you as being the last of Earth's Tegadelti, or as your father just said, maybe the first of their return."

"Tegadelti…interesting," Justice mused.

"It's time for you to go back, son," said his father. "No time to lose on your mission. Just remember you can always come visit us here. And we'll all be watching you and cheering for you."

"One more thing to keep in mind as you go back down," Sanite started, and paused looking at her other son, Eric, and her husband, as if weighing whether she should reveal the most important secret to Justice. Some kind of silent message of assent and approval passed among the three as Justice tried to gauge what was so important that his mom was vacillating on failing him.

"Well, Black, my dear, two things really. One, you've already figured out for yourself, obviously, since we are talking to one another right now. And that is that we -- our souls -- are immortal. We, humans, we do go on."

"Yes ma," said Justice gravely. "I have come to that conclusion already. "

"Good! The second thing is that that whole thing on the planet -- that whole racial inequality thing, social injustice, police brutality, slavery, oppression, fear, terror, war, hatred, poverty, death, disease…all of the various manifestations of human suffering and depravity…every tiny bit of it on planet Earth, or in the Milky Way or in the Laniakea Supercluster – all of it is fake! It is all a simulation, son. Every last bit is a part of a big old fractal simulation! It's all simulated. It's all simulation, inside simulation. inside simulation inside…. you get the point. All of it is one big old multifractal simulation setup!"

Justice sat down.

Sanite also sat down.

All four family members were now seated.

"BJ", Eric called his brother's attention.

"Yes?"

"Have you ever heard of the Zimbardo Experiment?"

"Can't say I have." Justice started to wonder where Eric was going with this.

"Let me cut this one to the chase for you," said Justice's father. "A psychologist named Zimbardo carried out an experiment in which his subjects were split into two groups. The subjects were Stanford University students. Zimbardo divided them into prisoners and guards, and the latter were given a modicum of power over the former. Next thing you know, each group started to take its role very seriously. But more importantly, the 'guards' started getting power-drunk, started subjecting the 'prisoners' to unscripted abuses. The situation got so bad, Zimbardo's partner forced him to abort the whole experiment half-way through."

"Okay, but I'm not sure I see where you're going with this, sir."

"The point, son," Justice's father said, raising his right palm up to signal his son to be patient "is that after a few days living in that simulated condition, the students actually fully assumed their given roles.

"That simulation had somehow become their reality. They all forgot the whole thing was just an experiment, just a simulation, and more importantly that any of them could have put a stop to the whole shebang by declaring 'enough is enough!' and refusing to participate any further in that nonsense. But not a single subject stepped outside the 'matrix' despite knowing on a certain cognitive level that their 'matrix' was fake.

"Okay, but…"

Justice was interrupted by the palm-up stop signal.

"The thing your mom is trying to reveal to you is that every social construct is just a simulation of a simulation of a simulation. It's all a simulation, son. Every bit of the whole thing is part of one giant multifractal universal simulation. The stupid tyrants on earth, the oppressed peoples, the racists, the anti-racists, the slaves, the so-called masters. Every last one of them is nothing but a simulacrum unit inside a big old simulation machine.

"All of this, all of us, Amma, the Afenifere, the Kaminani -- every last thing is part of an intricate machinery of simulation and meta-simulation. Yes, up to a point, the pain, the suffering, the power, the fame, the oppression, the wealth, the poverty, the births, the diseases, the deaths, up to a point, they are real...inside the matrix.

"But the minute you recognize the whole set-up for what it 'really' is, a part of you will begin to dissolve; the programmed, fear-based part of you will begin to dissolve, only to make room for a brand-new life-giving and unstoppable force of nature.

"Once you fully understand this idea, you become a true spark of God which is what everyone was originally before they all started assuming or accepting their different roles -- much like Zimbardo's subjects -- in the one single universal game of God."

"Dad, whoa!" Justice's turn to display the palm-up stop signal. The father smiled; like father, like son.

"It's all true," Sanite piped in.

"So why are we all living life so desperately then? Why are we all so much at each other's throat?"

"Amusement." Sanite answered.

"Whose amusement?"

"Yours and God's" Sanite dead-panned.

"God is amused by all this? That makes no sense at all, Ma."

"Rogue," Eric said quietly. "Look at Hollywood, Nollywood, Bollywood. Screenwriters, actors, producers, directors, casting agents, movie theaters, DVD manufacturers, stunt people, TV manufacturers, set designers, costume designers, gaffers, insurance companies...All of them participate in offering up entertainment. They know it's all for entertainment. We know it's all for entertainment. But that has never stopped any participants from giving everything they got. And knowing it's all make-believe has never stopped the average movie-goer from feeling angry, sad, or scared, and rooting for this character or that character -- if only for the two hours while that particular movie is playing. And yet, it's all maya...all of it, every little bit of it is part of a grand old illusion!"

"You're telling me we are all participants in a movie, and that a God is just sitting up there watching our production?"

"And eating a little popcorn," Eric said laughing at his own joke.

Justice got very pensive, looking all the way through to infinity.

At last -- when his mom was just about to rouse him -- Justice drew a long shuddering breath and said flatly, "Very well then. if an actor I must be, then let me star in the greatest epic of all."

"And what would that be son?" Sanite asked, concern sprinkled all over her voice.

Justice eyes became reptilian. To Sanite, he looked ready to nictitate. But he did not. He merely said, barely above a whisper, "Hannibal 2.0"

HIs family appeared to all instantly understand what Justice meant by that.

He embraced his family and made ready to leave.

"One more thing," Sanite said, as if as an afterthought.

"What's that, Ma?"

"Grandchildren, son," she smiled, pleading with her eyes. "I need some grandchildren to spoil!"

Justice shook his head and smiled.

"Alright, Ma. I'll see what I can do."

Justice turned and left the auditorium.

He never looked back. He didn't want his family to see the tears welling up in his eyes.

"Do come back and see us soon," Sanite shouted after him.

He   nodded   without   looking   back.

Justice was escorted out of the auditorium by Enoch and Elijah into a shimmering amber-colored translucent tunnel.

After a few steps into the tunnel, Amma materialized in person behind the three men.

"Gentlemen," Amma said softly as she stepped close enough to the three, "if you don't mind, I'd like to walk him through the tunnel."

Enoch and Elijah nodded, bowed and returned to the auditorium.

"Ms. Amma," Justice greeted as he noted the fact that the woman looked even more astounding in person than in the hologram version. He instinctively narrowed his eyes to protect his mind from the shock of having to stretch and wrap itself around such perfection of beauty without snapping.

"Justice" Amma began softly, "I'm breaking an untold number of rules and protocols right now by meeting with you in person."

Justice stood still, giving her his undivided attention, which he recognized in any case that in her presence, no other choice of attentional tribute was possible.

"We know that your family just now gave you some information about the simulation --the God-movie -- as they put it.

"What they told is what they know. That is all everyone back there in that auditorium currently knows. But that's only half the story."

"There is more?" Justice asked, not sure how much more he could take.

"Yes, there is more. Infinitely more! Think of what they just shared with you as being merely a static two-dimensional view of a dynamic, ever-evolving infinite-dimensional phenomenon."

"I'm not sure I understand your meaning, Ms. Amma."

"Think of it this way: if God is merely being passively amused as a solo but grand movie audience of the Universe, then actors and movie-people are in control of everything.

"A better way to understand what is really going on is to imagine two teams: TeamGod and TeamSatan. I'm using these terms very loosely, but you get the idea. God is the manager and coach of one team, and Satan is the manager and coach of the other. How each person or group of persons plays the game of life depends on whether the person is playing for TeamGod or TeamSatan.

"Funny thing is that by mutual agreement, the game is already rigged in favor of God. Eventually, no matter what, TeamGod wins, and TeamSatan always loses. No draw. Not even close. Your wonderful fellow human, Albert Einstein, once said, 'God doesn't play dice with the Universe!' If he only knew!" Amma smiled warmly. "Justice, please know that not only does God play dice with the Universe, He plays with loaded dice. And He absolutely plays to win! But we never shared that secret with Einstein.

"However, the game is also rigged to look temporarily as if TeamSatan is winning. So, most weak-willed and short-sighted people are tempted to play and root for TeamSatan.

"Temporarily?" Justice asked. "How temporary is temporarily?"

"It depends on a lot of factors," Amma answered, trying to gauge and calibrate just how much revelation of core divine secrets Justice's mind could handle without overclocking.

"Such as?" Justice pushed.

Such impatience and impudence, Amma mused silently, pursing her lips. "Such as the number of people involved in a given situation, in what, at what level of severity, for how long and so on. So is it a person? A family? A company? A political class? A gang? A nation? A group of nations? A planet? Etc. So it may take an hour, a day, a year, a decade, a lifetime, a century, even a millennium and so on for TeamGod to come out on top, and for TeamSatan to totally crash. But no matter how long or short the game, the end-result is set in stone: TeamGod always wins -- no matter how long TeamSatan appears to be winning.

"Does everyone belong to one team or the other? Are there any spectators?" Justice had to know.

"Every individual or group must belong to one team or the other as soon as they are old enough to have a conscience. Now it is extremely important to remember that even members of the same family or company or nation can absolutely belong to the opposing teams. Thus a TeamSatan parent may have a TeamGod child, and vice versa; a TeamGod executive may have a TeamSatan employee, and vice versa; a TeamGod President may have many TeamSatan citizens, and vice versa. It is under these conditions that team loyalty is most acutely tested vis-a-vis family loyalty or company loyalty or patriotism. Same with religious groups, ethnicities, and so on! Most groups are never homogeneous. So, never be afraid to disagree completely and uncompromisingly with your family, or friends, or co-workers or company leaders, or country leaders, or fellow ethnic group-members, for they are the ones most likely to drag you to hell with them."

"So, no spectators, no innocent bystanders, onlookers…you know, the uncommitted?"

"As soon as they've grown a conscience, everyone becomes a member of one team or the other by choice, or by default. And the way it works is simple; whosoever does not actively join TeamGod automatically becomes a member of TeamSatan by default. No spectators allowed -- except for little children whose consciences have not yet developed."

"So the default setting is TeamSatan."

"Yes."

"Can a person, group, a company, or a nation switch teams at will?"

"It happens all the time. But…" Amma paused, and seemed to stare off into space for what became an uncomfortably long time for Justice.

"But what?" he finally reeled her back in.

"People switch teams all the time. But they find it so much easier to join TeamSatan than to join TeamGod. To switch from TeamSatan to TeamGod is like climbing up the face of a mile-long greased sheer cliff. Now if you fall off the face of that cliff, it is infinitely harder to climb all the way back to the top. That's why the recruiters for TeamSatan always recruit first and foremost from amongst the young, arrogant and stupid.

"Once TeamSatan catches them young, inertia takes over as they slide down the surface of life's cliff, having fun and yodeling all the way down until they crash into the heap of other losers at the bottom of the mountain."

"So, people, companies, nations and such never make it back up to the very top?"

"Rarely. Very rarely. The will, the energy, the focus and the time required tends to frighten those who would like to. And yet…" Amma started to switch on the infinity gaze again. But this time, Justice reeled her back into the conversation quicker.

"And yet what?" He asked.

"And yet, the ultimate secret to winning the game of life is to actually struggle blood-drop by blood-drop up that cliff, clawing one's way up from the abyss where TeamSatan is, to the very summit where life's ultimate heroes -- that is, where the members of TeamGod -- gather to jubilate and celebrate…and start planning their very next climb."

"Next climb?!" Justice's eyes widened.

"Son, the climbing never ends. It is infinite. But you get stronger and more sure-footed with each effort, and the reverse is also true for the falling. As soon as they crash-land on one base camp, they slip and hurtle down to a new low. That's why no matter how low an individual has sunk; even though it is hard to do, it is also best for that individual to just up and begin his or her ascent at once, no matter how futile the prospect looks. Even if the effort kills the person, if his final act is cut short by death, as long as the final will, the final thought, the final act is an earnest effort to switch to TeamGod the person has a better chance in the next phase of humanity's immortal evolutions."

"Jesus Christ!" Justice exclaimed

"Well, I've never been called that before," Amma smiled. Her face lit up with the warmth of a thousand suns.

"Wow!" Justice exclaimed again, at a loss for words.

"Yes," Amma said. "That's it. All of the secrets to the whole shebang. The rest is mere details."

"Thank you," was all Justice could think to say.

"One last thing…" Amma started.

"What's that?" Justice asked before Amma could assume the infinity gaze.

"Start working on getting your mom the birthday present she wants."

"What's that?"

"Grandchildren, son. Grandchildren!"

Justice's mouth opened. No words came out.

Amma dematerialized. No farewell. No Godspeed. Nothing. Just poof! Gone. Just like that.

Justice had questions. He wanted to know more about God, about Satan, these ultimate team managers, these ultimate team owners. How were they faring? How, where, what, why… The idea of answering the endless chain of questions was probably   why   Amma   bailed   out   on   him.

Justice stepped outside the tunnel into what looked like the waiting area of the Intensive Care Unit of the John Henrik Clarke Hospital.

Seated in the waiting area were four people, three of whom looked strangely familiar, but somehow different from the way he remembered them.

One woman, one man, and two little girls.

Justice did not know the woman, but he soon recognized the man as Dr. Randall Robinson, the psychiatrist, and the two little girls were Brenda and Brandee.

Justice watched Dr. Robinson get up and walk briskly toward him. The man, Justice noted, now walked with a new spring in his step. He was beaming, which made Justice wonder why the man was so happy.

"It's great to have you back old friend!" Dr. Robinson, ignoring the dictates of professional reserve. "They tell me your surgery was an unqualified success!"

"Surgery?" Justice looked mystified.

Dr. Robinson pointed to the wound dressing that Justice had not realized until then that he was wearing.

"You banged your head up pretty hard during the melee."

"Melee?"

"Yeah…Remember when they came for you, and you tried to fight your way out of the premises?"

"Vaguely," Justice felt like a man just awakening from a dream within a dream.

"Well, within a few hours after Kim Chul-Moo launched his nukes, all hell broke loose all over the world. And the next thing we knew, some Tier-One type Special Operators stormed our hospital. And between you and them, you all darn near turned our facility into Mogadishu -- straight out of Black Hawk Down! But, a lot has happened all over the world in the three weeks you were out."

"Three weeks?!" Justice asked Dr. Robinson, looking at Brandee, Brenda, and the quiet lady for some kind of confirmation. All three nodded.

"Happy Martin Luther King Day!" said Brandee.

"Martin Luther King Day? What happened to Christmas, New Year…?"

"I'll fill you in later," said Dr. Robinson. He pointed at the kids. "The girls you already know, but let me introduce you to my boss. Dr. Black Justice, please say 'Hello' to Ms. Olutimilehin Elaine Brown, the Founder and CEO of Moremi Ventures.

"Ms. Brown, may I present Dr. Black Justice."

"You look human," said Ms. Brown, smiling, as she extended her hand for a handshake.

"I am human, ma'am," Justice shook the proffered hand. "But if I may say so, you, on the other hand, look absolutely divine." He finished, matching her smile.

"Why, thank you. It may interest you to learn that in the past three weeks, your humanity has been the subject of heated debates everywhere all over the world."

Justice looked at Dr. Robinson and at Brenda and Brandee. All three nodded.

"We met the President," Brenda said following the line of random information peculiar to children.

"Yes," Brandee piped in. "No one could figure out where he came from. They said he just stepped out of the ladies' restroom over there." She pointed to the restroom at the end of the waiting area.

"They said the President came out soon after a Black lady had gone in there. And they still haven't found the woman who went in there first. Some say she came here inside the Marine One -- you know, the Presidential helicopter -- when they first arrived here. But she disappeared from the bathroom after the President came out of there. Kinda creepy, you know? And what was the President doing in the female restroom anyway? Ewww! That's even creepier!" Brandee made a face.

"But we met him." said Brenda, "and he bought up all the cookies we could sell, and we won the contest. He also told us that the future of the country and of the whole world would depend on us. He told us to study hard…and to be good…even harder! I still don't understand what he means by that. But anyway, we are the cookie champions of the world now!" The girls gave each other high fives and hugs.

The three adults exchanged smiles.

"I should have known you girls had snuck up here with Dr. Robinson," said Nurse Ariel bursting into the waiting room.

"We called Code Adam looking for you all over the hospital!" She marched to where the girls were seated, giggling. Her face spelled relief as she put her arms at akimbo, and ordered the girls to get up and follow her to the kids' Oncology unit.

"Bye, Dr. Robinson, Mr. Justice and Ms. Brown!" The two girls piped as they got up and followed the nurse out.

Then Brandee turned on the nurse saying, "Ms. Ariel, you should be nice to us, you know? The President said we would be the future of the world!"

"That may be so, ladies," Nurse Ariel countered, "But the future of immediate concern right now is that you're both safely situated in your unit."

The nurse found a phone and called off the Code Adam. Children found! Another crisis resolved. Life went on at the John Henrik Clarke Hospital.

Justice pointedly looked at Dr. Robinsons newly sprouted hair. His features turned quizzical: "You," he said, "'the girls…hair…" he left the question unasked.

Dr. Robinson beamed. " A miracle! A real miracle. Cancer gone! Same for the kids, everyone. Every cancer patient. Total overnight remission. Oncologists are scratching their heads bloody all over the world, burnishing old resumes, looking for openings in other specialties!"

"No more cancer?" Justice tentatively asked.

"No more cancer!" Dr. Robinson affirmed.

"All that since I've been…out?"

"Past three weeks -- a global phenomenon!" Dr. Robinson's face strained to contain his joy.

"Alright, you boys," said Ms. Brown, "I suggest you make time to play catch-up later. There's something I need to discuss with Mr. Justice here before the press descends on him."

"No problem. I'll be in my office if you need me," Dr Robinson said, taking his leave.

As soon as the doctor was out of the waiting area, Ms. Brown said, "I have researched your background BJ. You don't mind if I call you BJ, do you?"

"BJ is good."

"Alright BJ. Call me Timi."

"Timi. Nice name."

"Why thank you! Listen up, BJ, I have reserved two very excellent eggs for you. Do you want them?"

"Eggs? Ms. Brown…Umm…Timi?" Justice sputtered.

"Yes, BJ! Eggs…as in the nice round and rubbery widgets that my ovaries love to manufacture. I have two of them reserved just for you. Once again, do you want them?" She was watching his face turn all shades of red-tinged black, and she reveled in his utter discomfiture.

"Two 'eggsellent' eggs," she said, dead panning, as she phonemized out the word 'excellent'. "Going once…going twice…"

"Wait, just wait! Let me try to make sense of what you're saying please!"

"Tick-tock, BJ. Tick-doggone-tock! I don't play social games. I find out what I want; I go for it. I plan to marry you. And I intend to have two sets of twins for you; two boys, two girls. All from two very good eggs. Do you want them or not? Tick-tock, tick-tock…"

"Wait! Yes! I mean yes, but…"

"No ifs, ands or buts. I like binary. I made my first billion in software systems -- very binary. Sir, do you want me and my darn good eggs? Yes? Or no?

"Yes ma'am…I mean Timi. Yes, of course. But this is all very highly unusual. I mean, has the world changed that much since I have been out?"

"Not in that sense," Timi replied. "It's just my way of going after what I want. I never want much in life -- only the best. Or nothing at all.

"And from all I've read and heard about you, you're the best darn man there is -- maybe the best darn man there ever was. And, since you happen to be in my hospital, I pulled some strings to be the first lady to get your attention before the competition wakes up!"

"Well, Timi, thank you! I hope this is not some very elaborate prank, but I think I'm beginning to like…love you too. It's crazy, but it feels natural. Whole. Complete!"

"Ata-boy, BJ! Fast learner! MIT, huh? Good job! But you ain't seen nothing yet. Wait till you see what a perfect friend and wife to you, and perfect mom for your twins I'll be, it'll blow your freaking mind right off!"

"Twins? This is so crazy! Twins! How do you know our kids will be twins?"

"See? Did you hear that? You just said 'our kids'! So, a part of you already knows I'm right. Anyway, I know they will be two sets of twins. Two boys, two girls. You'll see."

"Look, Timi, I may not be who you think I am. I'm very different from other guys, and I have some very critical, possibly suicidal, missions coming up. Maybe you want to rethink this whole twin business."

"Not on your life, buddy. You're not slipping that easily out of my grasp. You're mine. And I'm taking you back home with me. My chopper is on the roof. Waiting. Let's go! I'll get Dr. Robinson to fill out all the official discharge paperwork and stuff."

"Very well, then. Let's roll!" he said and pulled her close, and delivered a long, nothing-held-back kiss.

When she caught her breath, she said, "See? It's a game of hide-and-seek. While your mind is busy hiding, your heart is already busy seeking. That's why the heart finds while the brain lags behind. BJ, you and I are rare specimens. It's even rarer that we should find each other. I love you BJ!"

Justice held Timi by the shoulders at arm's length. He recalled his mom's and Amma's words about grandchildren. Everything seemed to be aligning but his heart skipped as he said words he had never said to a female companion before, "I love you, Timi!"

Just four words. He said them. And as soon as he had done so, he felt a deep spiritual shift on the path of his life. He couldn't explain it. He didn't want to explain it. But he knew he felt like a brand new person. More complete. More...whole. Like a yang that has found his yin.

They went up to the rooftop from where the waiting chopper took them to Hartsfield International Airport in Atlanta.

From there, Timi had a chauffeur drive Justice to The Westin Peachtree Plaza Hotel where she already had a suite reserved for him.

"I'll call you," she said, as they parted at Hartsfield.

"I don't have a phone," Justice replied.

"I know. I already had them stick a phone in your care-pack in your hotel suite. I'll call you around 4PM."

"Sounds good."

"And don't worry. I'll make all the wedding arrangements. Two weeks, max. Then we'll see whether you like your eggs omelets or sunny side up!" She said, taking in the look on his face, and bursted out laughing.

He too started to chuckle. The next thing he knew, he was matching her laughter, peal for peal, like two giddy teenage love-birds, right there at the Helipad at Hartsfield.

They left the airport in two separate Chevrolet Suburban SUVs, she to her mansion in Buckhead, and he to his reserved suite at the Westin Peachtree Plaza Hotel.

The last thought on Justice's mind before he drifted off to sleep was, "God, if only everyone could just be as straightforward, plain-dealing and as efficient as Timi, what a different world this would be!"

Timi was post-modern in love and dating, but extremely old-fashioned with intimacy.

Other than their passionate kiss at first blush in the ICU waiting room at her hospital, Timi declined all invitations by Justice to visit him in his hotel room.

She went shopping for him, bought him Nigerian, Arab and Italian outfits and shoes, and sent them daily to his hotel suite. Each package always arrived with an extra Nike outfit.

The woman, it seemed to Justice, was crazy about the Nike brand, and she made sure Justice did not forget it. When he had finally caved and asked about the Nikes, she had laughed and said, "I always try to support companies that show some decent moral standards, and I have regarded Nike as a brave and moral company ever since they started supporting Colin Kaepernick, at a time when no other company wanted to be associated with him. I do have my favorites in almost every category: The Intercept, The Guardian and The Independent, all three news outlets; Netflix, TikTok, K-Pop stans, Anonymous, Black Lives Matter, of course; Quakers, Dropbox, Greg Popovich, LeBron, Kaepernick, Milwaukee Bucks, Lakers, Clippers, Bill and Melinda Gates Foundation, Richard Branson and his Virgin Group and Ben & Jerry's. Did I mention Ben & Jerry's? Okay, hint, hint, hint, BJ! Maybe your bride-to-be actually loves Ben & Jerry...Know what I mean? I mean, you know, not quite as much as I love you, of course, but I'm warning you, lover-boy, those two guys are your hottest competition now!" She laughed with unrestrained joy.

She home-cooked for him three times a day, every day.

Every evening before going to bed, they called each other for a nightcap on Microsoft Teams. Those encrypted video chats were the highlight of their days.

Two weeks after their first meeting, the wedding took place, a very small and private affair at the Morehouse College Martin Luther King, Jr. International Chapel.

Somehow, Timi had made arrangements for Dr. Robinson to be the best man, Brenda and Brandee to be the flower-girls and Robert Smith, a philanthropist and friend and mentor to Timi, and an alumnus of Morehouse College served as the Father of the Bride.

But the honeymoon was the crown jewel.

Timi had splurged on a full-service honeymoon rental of the whole of Necker Island -- a lushly verdant well-appointed piece of paradise tucked away in the British Virgin Islands.

Nuptial intimacy on wedding night revealed in no uncertain terms to Justice how truly old–fashioned his bride was, and how perfectly fitting it was that she had deliberately planned to celebrate her honeymoon in the Virgin Islands.

On their way back home to Atlanta, Georgia, Timi and Justice both agreed that the fireworks and tectonic quakes of their wedding night were to be eternally repeated and powered by the pure fuel of their love. And they were sealed as a couple and as a family.

As soon as they settled in and freshened up from the long flight home, Timi invited Justice to join her in their cozy den.

"Honey, check this out," Timi said, laughing as Justice sauntered into the room. She was trying to lift a huge rose-colored bottle that was stamped with a deeper rose-colored ace-of-spades symbol.

"What's this?" Justice hefted the bottle onto the table.

"A crazy wedding gift from my cousin, Jay Z."

"Jay Z? You mean the…"

"Yup, he tells me we're second-and-a-half cousins. Crazy Jay Z!" She laughed infectiously. Justice joined her in the laughter for no other reason than that her laughter made him happy.

"But, what is it?" he persisted.

"It's a 2013 Armand de Brignac Rose Midas. It's champagne Sweetie. Sham-pain, my love!" She had a way of phonemizing her words to make the ordinary sound weird and funny. "And it costs over a quarter-million dollars per bottle!" She bursted out laughing.

"Well, let's drink to Da J-Hova, Jay Z!" said Justice.

"As we buzz out to Da Blue Mother Queen Bey!" said Timi, feeling tipsy with love already. "Hey Google, play 'Crazy in Love' by Beyoncé!"

"Serve up, drink up, honey. Have a sat. There is stuff I need to tell you." Timi said.

"Uh-oh!" Justice looked at his bride, and braced up. He sat down across from her. "What's wrong my queen?"

"Nothing. Nothing at all. Everything is absolutely perfect." Timi paused "I wish I could just bottle this moment, and sip on it for the rest of our lives."

"Nothing wrong with that. But something is bothering you," Justice pressed. "What is it?"

"I bugged you!" Timi blurted out.

"You bugged me? What do you mean?"

"I bugged you, because I am crazy in love with you…Or maybe it's the other way around: Maybe I am crazy in love with you because I bugged you! I don't know which came first any more!" Timi sounded exasperated.

"Timi, please relax. And talk to me. Tell me what's going on, please."

"Okay, BJ. Okay. First things first: I totally love you, and I totally love everything about you. I am hopelessly absolutely in love with you."

"The feeling is obviously mutual, Timi. But, what do you mean you bugged me? I never felt bugged by you."

Timi half-stood up, leaned across the coffee table and planted a kiss squarely on Justice's kiss-worthy lips.

"Oh, you poor, innocent little warrior hubby-bubby. You drive me totally crazy in love!"

"Poor, innocent little warrior?"

"Yes, BJ, that's you! That's all of you! You're so cool! So innocent! All warrior. All man! No guile."

"Timi, I love you, but right now, I have no idea what you're talking about."

"Honey, I'm talking about Gorgon Brain. And about Godium. And about Gamma Ray Bursts. And about CRISPR'ed viral vectors!"

Justice sat straight up, eyes narrowing for better focus. Queen Bey had stopped buzzing on Google Home. Total silence in the house. No pin dared drop.

"What do you know about Gorgon Brain and Godium?" Justice asked

"More than you do," Timi said softly, sighing.

She carefully placed her champagne flute on the mahogany coffee table. The bubbles raced one another playfully to the top of the drink. The hushed celebration of each bubble's ascent was the only sound in the room

"I created them. I designed them. You, my love, may have been the father of Gorgon Brain, But I -- I was, and I am, still the mother of that machine. Yes, Gorgon Brain was built completely based on your doctoral work at MIT. I read your thesis, and I was floored. Utterly floored by it. I'm known in Silicon Valley and on Wall Street as the Black Athena. I had never met any man whose mind could match mine…until I came across your thesis. It was a work of stupendous genius. The more I studied it, the more I realized, I had finally met my match.

"So, I attacked it and attacked it and attacked it all alone every night after my regular job at the NSA. It took me a couple of years, but I never backed down.

"Finally, I was rewarded; I found a single flaw buried deep in the heart of your algorithm. And then, I pounced!

"I quit my job at the NSA, spent another two years building a prototype. When I was done, I offered Gorgon Brain to Uncle Sam. I still had contacts at the NSA. I called the right people who called the right people to finally get someone at the top to ink my contract into something known as the Black Budget…an untraceable governmental expenditure. They gave me a contract worth tens of billions. In return, I gave them Gorgon Brain, just exactly as you designed it. Except for one difference.

"I had had an epiphany: I realized you had deliberately placed the hidden flaw in your algorithm as a backdoor for possible future exploits. Somewhat like a Trojan Horse. You built for yourself a capacity to go in in the future, and take control of the system, if you ever needed to. Double genius, my God! Genius enough to create that algorithm. And even greater genius to deliberately hide a 'flaw' in it, the same way nature hides a 'flaw' in a diamond to make it sparkle even brighter!

"So, instead of fixing your Trojan horse, I left it alone just as you wrote it.

"But I added my own little honeypot algorithm to it inside the shadow of your backdoor, I wrote a one-way-mirror code so I could watch you…or whoever else had enough brainpower to exploit your 'bug' in the future.

"So, when you came to pwn the roofkit, you triggered an alarm in my honeypot. And that was when I started monitoring the type of people and data that you in turn were monitoring. I was watching you watching them.

"I saw what you were doing with CRISPR and the viral vectors. How you were targeting the DNA of racists, bullies and tyrants everywhere.

"I put two and two together and realized you were planning to make bad people literally become the very victims they were abusing or had abused in the past. Police officers, judges, politicians, lawyers, recruiters, college admissions officers, career counselors, correction officers, doctors, property managers, mortgage lenders, abusive husbands, bankers, teachers, CEOs, Human Resources people, a whole army of bad people who all thought they'd gotten away with abusing others.

"Once I saw the type of information you were collecting and collating, I fell in love completely with you. I knew then, as I now know for sure, that not only are you the most brilliant man I know, but that you are also the most exacting with your sense of justice and honor.

"So, as you continued to track and infect bad guys with your Judgement Day Virus, I continued to track you.

"The day you discovered Godium was the first time I've ever been afraid in my whole life. I strongly suspected that if some so-called powerful person ticked you off, you might deploy Godium."

"You were afraid I would blow up the world?"

"Hell, no!" Timi said, surprising both of them with the sharpness of her tone. "No honey. Hell, I have wanted to blow the damned world up many times myself. And there are many more like us out here. Only difference is that they have not discovered Godium. But you and I have."

"So, then what were you afraid of?"

"BJ, I was scared spitless that I would never get a chance to meet you and to fall in love with you, and to make sweet love to you, and to have twins for you before you end the world."

"That's all you were afraid of?"

"Yep. And boy, did that prospect scare the spit out of me.

"Then I noticed you started tracking information about psychiatrists who had experience with hostage negotiations. I already owned the John Henrik Clarke Hospital at Igbo Landing anyway, and several other healthcare facilities across the nation, so I quickly put an irresistible package together for Dr. Randall Robinson and literally forced him to drop everything and join us at Clarke. And I sealed the deal for him by semi-promising that by joining us, he would have a chance to take part in the greatest hostage crisis negotiation in history once he joined us, I planted his resume all over LinkedIn and Gorgon Brain for your viewing pleasure. I set up a honeypot inside a honeypot for you, honey!" She slapped her own thigh, and burst out laughing.

"And then, I sat back and watched you walk into it all"

"So, the doctor, the hospital, all that was a set-up?"

"Yes. And you, my love, are worth every last bit of it!" She smiled, got up and kissed him again.

"I also researched your taste in women. You like the straight up, take-charge, plain– dealing, hundred-percent committed type. Thankfully, I was already all that and more."

"But I had to bone up some on the home-cooked meal deal part. At least, I haven't fed you any burnt offerings so far, have I?" she asked coyly.

"No honey, it's been really all very delectable. But if you want me to, I can take over the cooking for us, you know."

"No babe," Timi got all coquettish, "Let's do the cooking together. The kitchen will then become an anteroom to our bedroom. First, we get cooking; then we really get cooking!" She winked at him and laughed her cathedral-peal laughter.

"Okay. Sounds great. So, then, you eventually showed up at the hospital on Martin Luther King Day to literally sweep me off my feet," Justice prompted.

"Heck no! I didn't wait to just swoop in and catch my prize. I was very busy putting every piece of the final showdown together. I orchestrated everything to a T."

"I had to spend some enormous call-in-favors to get the White House to agree to the raid on the hospital. No live ammo allowed. And the President had to agree to show up during the mission. He was extremely reluctant to be seen in public looking like your mom, and all that! But when I promised him that that was the only way to get him back to being the good old Richard Tate, he jumped on board.

"And those soldiers who came to capture you? They were highly paid Hollywood stuntmen -- all, except for three former Delta Force guys who owed me a favor. The DBoys choreographed and coordinated the whole hospital raid scenario. They predicted exactly how you were going to react because they have Delta training like you. Their mission was to stun and capture you for me!"

"Holy Jesus, Timi! There were Delta guys involved?"

"Yup." Timi made an innocently apologetic face, and dipped her neck forward, as if to say, "S-o-r-r-y!"

"I could have killed them. And they could have killed me. No ammo necessary. We're Delta...we can kill someone with a doggone piece of toilet paper if we had to!"

"They could have died. True. But you...no way. Part of the mission specification was to protect you with their very lives if necessary. Trust me honey. You know Delta. And when I worked NSA, I also knew these particular operators; they would have died for you, and for me."

"Okay. Then, what about how any stressors that affected my heart rate could have detonated the Godium and caused the Gamma Ray Burst to activate"

"Not likely, Sweetie-pie. The world will not end...not until you give me my two sets of twins!" She burst out laughing, this time, she laughed on behalf of the two of them because Justice had his mouth open, but no sounds came out.

Eventually, he said, "I rigged my dead man's switch to activate upon undue stress."

"And I, Mrs.Olutimilehin Elaine Justice deactivated that switch a long time ago -- on the very day I fell in love with you -- on August 15th, over two years ago to be exact. I took necessary precautions to make sure you will marry me before the world ends. I even recruited your mom in my mission!"

"What?!"

"They don't call me Black Athena for nothing! But frankly, I think what they freaking ought to do is they freaking need to start calling Athena, White Timi. I am not a Black anybody; she is the white me, not the other way round." Peal of laughter.

"Never mind about Black and white, Timi or Athena. What do you mean you recruited my mom in your mission?"

"I set up two simulacra in the hospital. One simulacrum was for President Tate. The other simulacrum was for you."

"Simulacrum?"

"Yeah, you know, c'mon…like AI-simulations of real people, places, things, processes or events."

"One for me, and one for Tate?"

"Yeah. I managed to convince Tate that the only way we could switch his body and mind back to being the old Tate was to experience the simulacrum designed and programmed specifically for him." She paused to gauge Justice's attention. He was good.

"I set his simulacrum up to let him see and experience the whole world slowly vaporizing before his eyes, so that he would see the suffering and hear all the screams as he became the last person left in the world before he too slowly vaporized from the feet up. A total nightmare simulation. So, when they concussed you guys -- well, you and Tate, who had the appearance of your mom at the time -- when both of you got stunned, we moved you both up into the simulacra chambers set up for you in the ICU."

"And what then about your mission and my mom?"

"As you know already, in Silicon Valley, at Singularity University, we have technologies that will easily take five, ten years before the rest of the world hears about them."

"So, what about my mom?"

"I made her simulacrum to appear to you and ask you for grandchildren." Timi said. No laughter this time. No smiles even. Her eyes were searching Justice's face. Begging for forgiveness. Pleading for love's unconditional understanding.

"You created AI software to make my mom appear in my consciousness and ask me for grandchildren?"

"Yes." Timi knew things would go binary from here on, but she needed to package the whole truth together with her total crazy love for Justice. She didn't feel right holding anything back from him any longer. "Yes, I designed, programmed, and built the whole hardware, wetware, and software. I built the whole system to win the only love I've ever wanted, the only love I will ever want. Yes, I built your mom. I built a simulacrum of your mom to help me persuade you to give me your heart. I love you without any regrets. I love you with all my heart and all my life. I love you. I love all of you, body, mind and soul, BJ."

Justice gazed into infinity while looking at his wife. He kept very still, very silent.

Timi held her breath for what seemed like eternity.

"What about my brother, my dad, Enoch, Elijah, Tubman, Fela…What about Amma? What about all the other people in the auditorium with me and my mom? Did you engineer them as well?"

"What other people? What are you talking about BJ?"

"So you did not engineer Amma or Enoch or Tubman or Fela or anyone else?"

"Hell, no! Who are those? Do you have any idea how much computing resource I had to expend just to create your mom believably without any motion-induced pixelation or choppiness and the annoying Max-Headroom-type reverb effect? I could never do that to her. I could never do that to you. So, no. No extras. If I had added a second person, your unit would have sucked all available electricity in town and shorted. So, no. Who is Amma? Elijah? Tubman, you say? And a fella?"

"No. Fela…Fela Kuti. Harriet Tubman. Prophet Enoch. My dad. My brother. Prophet Elijah. And a goddess named Amma, who strangely enough, now that I think about it, looks identical to you!"

"Please, Black, please have a seat."

"Timi, I am seated. It's you who are standing up."

Timi looked around. "Yeah, you're right! I need to have a seat. Please tell me about all the other people you 'met'"

"Timi, are you sure you coded only my mom?"

"BJ, I promise you by the only love of my life that it is utterly impossible to code more than just your mom into that system. I'll show you the code; you can check it out for yourself."

"How then were you able to code other people into President Tate's simulacrum?"

"Easy! The objects who populated the world in his simulacrum never interacted with him at all. He simply observed the whole world of faceless individuals experiencing suffering and dissolution. And he only really felt just his own body and mind dissolving. All the others, he simply saw and heard. No interaction. Quite unlike the code for AI real-time interaction between you and your mom."

"And between me and all the other people in the auditorium. Amma, the goddess, even pleaded with me to give my mom some grandchildren -- birthday gifts, she called them!"

Timi reached for the bottle of champagne and took a straight swig.

"So, you didn't program the talk about Tegadelti, the grandchildren, TeamGod, TeamSatan, Afenifere or Kenimani?"

"No, BJ, I didn't. I couldn't even if I had any idea what you're talking about!"

"What about Tate? He showed up inside the auditorium. I briefly felt like ripping his throat out and feeding it to him. But I was learning so much astounding stuff, I felt it would be a total waste of my time and energy to kill a mocking president.

"And seeing mom, my brother and dad back there in the audience made me realize that people never really die anyway -- at least not those people I met in there anyway.

"This is crazy, Timi. This is freakier than anything I've ever handled."

"I'm struggling to wrap my mind around all these things you're telling me. The very NPCompleteness of the problem is more than enough to make Alan Turing's ghost break out in sweat. There's absolutely no way; it simply isn't technically feasible at this time to program and manipulate all that data in real-time in that module. Even if I had the time to do it, the simulacrum couldn't handle all that computation. It would have exploded, or simply melted down, crashed or frozen."

"But it all happened: and your module did not melt down. And then there is the issue of the cancer cure."

"What cancer? What cancer cure, honey?"

"Well Amma promised to wipe out cancers and stuff. And the next thing I know, I get back here and the three people I know who had cancers, their cancers are gone!"

"Which three people?"

"Brenda, Brandee, and Dr. Robinson. Or was that all also a set-up by you?"

"Set-up? By me? BJ, I promise you I have no idea what you're talking about."

"Okay Timi. I think this is bigger than a mere simulacrum. If what I'm thinking absolutely checks out, I think your machine may have opened up a portal to…to a new world, to a new dimension. I think your crazy-love obsession may very well have bought humanity a whole new lease on life."

"Humanity? New lease on life? BJ? Please, all I was after; all I was ever after is you. I just love you. And I wanted you…still want you to love me."

"But don't you see? I do love you. That goes without saying. But this situation is clearly above and beyond our love for each other. The fate of our world may very well be hanging on your simulacrum chamber."

"But how?"

"Well look at it this way: when you built it, you populated it with one individual whose sole job was to talk to me about grandchildren. Okay, for one thing she told me things that have nothing to do with grandchildren. She told me things such as the Tegadelti, they told me things about the Afenifere, the Kenimani. So, I didn't know about those things. But somehow the AI version of my mom knew…knows about them. How did that happen? And on top of that, my chamber got populated by individuals I never knew from Adam, mostly talking about stuff way above my pay-grade! And then cancer cures promised to me by Amma have already started to happen?!

"Honey, I think your simulacrum machine is way more than you think it is. I think it can give people hope. It can give their lives meaning, and it can give them a sense of community and direction. People need this machine, Timi!"

"I know. Even President Tate looked different when he came out of the chamber, even before his reconstitution inside that fake bathroom. He looked like a man who had just had a major epiphany. I didn't think much of it at the time! I was just waiting for you to get done."

"How did you know that I was ready to come out anyway?"

"Brain scan. You resumed normal activity patterns in your right parietal lobe. It showed us that your focus had shifted from a higher power or a higher purpose back to focusing on the self and on self-preservation. So, we turned down the activator in the chamber."

"Make this machine compact, easily programmable and portable like a personal computer or a smartphone, and make it cheap enough for every household, and you can change the world forever."

"I'll think about it. What about you? What are you going to do now?"

"Well I need to catch up first with all the stuff that happened while I was out of commission: the nukes that were shot by countries all going nuts; why the nukes never landed on earth despite the stabilization of Gorgon Brain by you and Amma, and now all these peace talks spearheaded by Tate. And speaking of Tate, what to make of all of these Presidential pardons and immunity crap he gave me. What did you put in his drink?"

"I told you he too must have experienced something inside that chamber beyond what I programmed for him to experience. I don't know…the man has become a sweet, doting little grandpa since he came back."

"Well, he still has to answer for what he and his son did to six of my men. I'm going to expose them. I'm going to talk him down -- if it's the last thing I do."

"Didn't you mention some mission-some larger-than-life purpose you picked up inside the chamber?"

"Yeah, I've got to lead the world in battle against the Kenimani."

"Well, in that case, don't you feel it would be better for you to have a subdued empathetic ally in the White House to give you access to global resources, honey?"

"Timi, this man and his son killed my men."

"Honey, I know. And believe me, I am deeply sorry for your loss. Please just consider this: you can avenge your men, and lose an ally in the White House, which can delay your preparations for your Kenimani missions. Or, you can use his guilt…and his knowledge of your deadly powers to your advantage. Keep him close by your side, and use him to serve a higher purpose for a better world. What would your men ask you to do, if they could speak on their own behalf right now? Honey, I don't know them, but I've heard it said for warriors to keep their friends close; and their enemies closer!"

"Yes," Justice looked at his wife with an expression closer to reverence than mere regular love. "Yes, Timi, you are right. I hate to admit it in this instance, but you are right. Sun Tzu, The Art of War: Keep your friends close, and your enemies closer!" But, then his face took on a look of fearsome intensity. "But the greatest advice ever given by Sun Tzu was to keep your wife closest!" And he pounced on her, and tickled her as she squealed with delight like a teenager. The more she squealed, the more mercilessly he tickled her until tears of love, laughter and soulmate-ship   were   rolling   down   both   of   their   cheeks.

Busy day all around. The Justices split things up.

Despite an abundance of help from her children, grandchildren and robo-servants, Timi chose to do most of the birthday preparations herself. She wanted to infuse her maternal touch. After all, it was not every day her first born twins turned 50.

As she busied herself fussing and lording it around her kitchen, she kept an ear out for the Presidential election results. This was an election unlike no other.

She had met two of the candidates the very same day she had met her husband.

Justice sauntered into the kitchen, rubbed the head of one of his grandsons, popped a grape in his mouth, hooked an arm around his wife's waist and gave her a light kiss.

His mind was still buzzing with the afterglow of the just concluded simulcast.

Over the last 50 years, Simulacra Corporation -- founded by the Justices -- had become a global phenomenon, a Fortune Five company on the brink of being one of the first Earth-based companies to be listed on the Inter-Galactic Stock Exchange.

From toddlers to the most senior citizens, everyone had a personal simulacrum chip-strip tattoo. Anyone was now able to connect to deep reality from anywhere just by voice –activating or biometricizing their headband chip-strip tattoo.

The simulcast which Justice had plugged in to watch while Timi cooked had just ended, but his mind was still abuzz with the afterglow effect.

And by the look on Timi's face, Justice could tell that she knew he wasn't quite fully back from the deep reality simulcast.

"What happened at the cast, honey?" she prompted.

He blinked, not quite sure where to begin.

"What did Amma say?"

"Not Amma this time, babe," Justice said, still struggling to collect his thoughts. "Not Amma this time."

"Wanna talk about it?"

1

"Let's do that…in the den." He applied subtle steering pressure to her waist, and Timi reluctantly abandoned her cooking and went with him as she called out, "Hey, Titilola-Ejide!"

The Justices' supermodel daughter-in-law answered, "Yes, mommy!"

"Do watch over the casserole for me, will you please, honey? And don't let your rambunctious twins distract you, please. Ain't no one looking to eat burnt offerings…again…today!"

"Mom! Are you ever going to forgive and forget that one single mishap, which happened like what…25 million years ago?" Titilola-Ejide, a beautiful woman in her forties, responded.

"How can we ever forget that disaster? I still suffer acid reflux to this day as a result of that meal!"

Titilola-Ejide shook her head, rolled her eyes and sighed theatrically as she reached in a cabinet, pulled out a bottle and offered it to her mother-in-law, "Here, Ma…have some Rollaids!"

Timi smiled, ignored her daughter-in-law's offer, and followed her husband into the den.

As they settled onto the sofa in the den, Justice said, "Five billion people tuned in today."

"Five billion?!"

"Not counting the pets."

"And Amma didn't say anything?"

"She spoke…only to say that she would not be speaking today. She had a special guest."

"Who was it?"

"God," Justice said flatly.

"The guest was introduced as God?" Timi probed.

'No, but judging by what the Guest said, that is the only conclusion I could reach without completely losing my mind."

"What did She or He say?"

2

"It was an all audio podcast, all audio, no video. I recorded it for you in case you want a direct listen?"

"No, I'm okay. You just give me the gist of it now. I'll listen to the whole thing later."

"Alright, no problem. By the way, one thing to note: everyone said they heard the Special Guest in the listener's own most deeply personal voice and favorite language of choice."

"So, you heard the speech in your own voice?"

"Yes," said Justice.

"So what did you hear?"

"It went something like this...so earnest...so casual; no brimstone and fire, no thunder and lightning. Just a relaxed and calm...calming, still, small voice. In my voice, He said:

'Greetings! By the way you reckon your time, it has been a while since I spoke to you as a group. For the past several millennia, I have restricted myself to talking to some of you once in a while on a one-on-one basis.

'But your guide -- Amma -- has done everything in her power to persuade me to speak to you as a group today.

'So here I am. You have Amma to thank for this occasion.

'I have observed that your world is all chaos, just as your individual lives are all one big old messy chaos.

'I feel sorry for you.

'The root cause of all your problems is two-fold:

'You do not know who you are.

'And not knowing who you are, you do not know what to do.

'Because of these two areas of ignorance, you rush about everywhere without any idea of your true identity, and without any compass to give you a sense of direction.

'And so, in your chaos, you destroy yourselves, you destroy one another and you destroy my world. My world! You have multiplied your inner and outer chaos.

3

'I have told you the solution in the past. And I have also sent several guides to remind you of the solution.

'But each time, you soon forget.

'You suffer racial amnesia.

'Your whole race has drunk too deeply from River Lethe. And so, you forget

' I feel sorry for you -- for the mess you have made of your lives, for the mess you have made of my world. I am saddened by your pain. I never wanted to see you hurt. I never wanted to see you suffer.

'But, here we are, I have to step in yet again to remind you of Who you are, and what your real job on Earth is.

'Once you regain your lost identity, and you remember your forgotten purpose, your lives and your world will be rid of all confusion, chaos and suffering.

'So, firstly, Who are you?

'For those of you who have loaded up on Google as part of your Akashapedia, please look up in the Holy Bible Genesis 1:27. Also Psalm 82:6, and John 10:34. It's in your Holy Quran, your Torah, your Veda, your Tripitaka. as well all of your other holy scriptures.

'Clearly, you have been told many times in so many messages I sent to you that you are Gods.

'I have sent messengers to proclaim that fact to you in all scriptures

'But, for some reason, because of your own head-strong, self-willed, petty reasons, you either ignore my messages, or you forget them as soon as your chaos-of-the-moment is resolved.

'I feel sorry for you; I feel sorry for you for all your self-imposed suffering.

'You are good because You are Gods. You are good, you are enough, you are complete because You are Gods.

'Now, you no longer know this merely from the scriptures or from the archeological and the cosmological evidence. Now I am proclaiming it directly directly to You:

'YOU ARE GODS!

4

'I made you in my own image. I placed a spark of me into you. That which you call your souls is the bit of Me in you. The rest of your body is merely a flesh and bone vehicle for your soul. Your soul is Me!

'But you do everything within your power to soil Our soul; to soil the Me in You!

'I feel sorry for you. You hurt so much; You suffer so much because You try so hard to soil Me!

'Please remember You are bits of Me, and I -- I am all of You.

'You are Gods!

'That is Your identity. Do not lose it ever again. And do not allow the identity-thieves of the soul to steal it from You. Guard it with your life, because it is your life. It is Me, and it is You, for We are One.

'You are Gods!

'Now that You remember who You are, let us remind You of what You are supposed to do.

'Look at your world. Look at your lives. Nothing but a whole lot of mess and chaos.

'You bemoan and you decry the chaos around you and within you.

'Why? Because you forgot yourself and your mission.

'I feel sorry for you. So, I will help you. I will remind you of your mission, your purpose.

'Remember We created order out of chaos, and We call it cosmos, which means order?

'Well, then, being that You, too, are Gods, don't you suppose it is in fact your job to create order out of your ongoing chaos?

'Do You remember now? Go ye, be fruitful and multiply? Have dominion? What did You think we meant? All we were telling You was to go out there and make the Second Law of Thermodynamics subject to your will, because you are Gods! You are supposed to reduce Entropy.

'That's your job. That is your purpose. In life that is your singular mission. Everything else is mere details.

'Your job, your mission is to identify your favorite part of chaos, and then to spend the rest of your natural life bringing order to rule the chaos.

'That it! That's all of it!

'Did you think there was more?

'Look at Our own record. That Is all We did. That is all We have ever done — always creating order out of chaos. But guess what? That is more than enough mission to last each of You multiple lifetimes

'So, now consider concrete examples.

'Say your country is passing unjust laws. That's chaos. if that is your kind of thing, go out and fight to expunge the unjust laws from the books.

'Say people around you are starving. That is chaos. If starving people bother you, maybe you can turn the chaos into a cosmos by teaching and practicing good agriculture.

'Maybe the chaos you dislike is ignorance, then you should consider educating yourself, and then trying to educate others.

'Perhaps diseases are the particular chaos that gets under your skin, then you may consider bringing some order into the chaos by studying medicine, nursing, pharmacy and other health sciences.

'Perhaps, slavery and oppression are the kinds of chaos that get your goad, then you may want to spend your life as a freedom-fighter.

'If it is noise that bothers you, try studying and playing music, or try practicing silence.

'As I have stated, your primary job is to replace chaos with order, that is, with cosmos: the specific steps you take to achieve your end are mere details; provided you make sure that in your effort to impose order in some area, you yourself are not guilty of creating chaos in some other areas.

'And so, to sum it all up for you, you are to remember that You are Gods, and that Your primary purpose in life is to create Your cosmos out of the chaos around and within You.

'And, here is the final secret:

'Ultimately, the most powerful tool at your disposal for creating a cosmos out of chaos is that thing which you call love.

6

'Love is your final answer. Once you understand that, and you learn to apply it as we do, your whole life, your whole world will become one well-ordered cosmos.

'Try Your best to love one another as much as We love You.

'I am Your standard. You have been told of Gold standards. But, your most important Standard is Me. I am your God Standard.

'But still You are Gods. And your sole focus in life is to compete lovingly with one another to see which among you can be crowned next to Us -- the Greatest God of All.

'You already compete in so many areas of entertainment to be the Greatest Of All Time in this or that field of endeavor: Baseball, Basketball, Singing, Acting, Running, Money-Making, Powerlifting, Nascar Racing, Football, Boxing, High Jump, Long Jump, Storytelling, Lawyering, Scientific Discovery, Child-Rearing, Debating, Computer Programming, Marketing…You name it; you compete already to be the greatest at it. You already compete in all things, except the one thing We sent You down to go compete in.

'All You ever have to do is through Your thoughts, through Your words and through Your deeds to lovingly compete to be the Greatest God of All. You should participate in that singular competition all throughout your life. Then, when You are done with each lifetime, You come home to Us for a little rest and recreation.

'Then, You go back down and resume the loving competition afresh as soon as You feel rested enough.

'That is, it. That is all of it.

'That is who You are. That is who We are. And that is what We do.

'Above all else, strive to love one another even as We love You.

'And We love You unconditionally because You are Us.'

"And then He clicked off," Justice took a deep breath.

"And then, what happened? Timi asked.

"Nothing. Silence. Total silence. Never heard anything like it. It was like the opposite of death, but if wasn't life either; it was something infinitely better. It was like the type of silence one would expect to experience in the final transition from total chaos to perfect order."

"What did Amma say after that?"

7

"Amma? I -- I guess nothing. What do you say after God has just finished speaking? No, Amma never came back online."

"My God! I missed all that?"

"And my Goddess, I recorded it all for Thee!"

Timi made a gesture like she was going to swat Justice with her spatula as the two burst out laughing.

"So, what did I miss?" Justice asked. "The elections. Looks like they've declared a winner."

"A total landslide," Timi piped. "It wasn't even close."

Justice flicked his head in the direction of the hologram that popped on cue in the den. The political analysts were having a field day.

"Looks like the Twins actually did it!" Justice beamed.

"Yes, sir! History in the making right here. The very first female Co-Presidents of the United States of America: Brandee Woolsley-Taylor and Brenda Taylor-Woolsley. It's the craziest thing. If I wasn't seeing this with my own two eyes, I'd label it a bad Hollywood movie. But here you have it: two ladies, one black, one white,, known each other since kindergarten, married to each other's older brother. Their moms were best friends. Now the two women and their VP husbands are going to run one of the most powerful nations in history! Only in America!"

Justice had gone very quiet and darkly pensive. It took a minute before Timi picked up on his somber mood.

"Honey," Timi's neck craned forward with concern, "Whoa, there! Honey, what's wrong?"

"I need to start preparing for their inauguration," Justice replied almost in a whisper.

"Yeah, I get that, but you don't sound too happy or too excited about the whole thing."

"I have to be ready," Justice said cryptically.

"For what honey?"

But he did not hear her. His mind was already visualizing the final moves of a 50-year   long   chess   match.

Fifty years ago, an uneasy truce had been struck between Black Justice on the one hand, and President Tate and his son, DI, on the other.

For mutual strategic reasons Justice and the President had known it was best for all parties involved to work together to eradicate systemic racism, injustice, police brutality, sexism, gender bias, religious tyranny and all other varieties of bigotry and oppression from the land.

Part of the unpublicized portion of their agreement was that DI had to return the Medal of Honor he had been awarded for his fake heroism. He also had to waive all benefits associated with his military veteran status.

Both the President and his son had grudgingly agreed to these conditions rather than have to be forced to deal with the outrage if Justice should ever be pushed to going public with the information he possessed.

Moreover, both men were well aware that assassinating Justice was not a viable option, based on their experience with his dead man's switch gambit.

They both knew that assassinating him would spell the end of the world. Justice made no effort to enlighten them otherwise.

So for five decades, they worked together in peace. It had been an uneasy peace -- but peace nonetheless.

From the heart of Dam Neck, Virginia, Justice with the help of other Tier-One veterans from Delta Force, SEAL Teams, PJ's and Marine Ghost Recon, had created a global force of space troopers named HELL.

The HELL warriors were like Spartans on steroids. Male and female, they were trained in 18-year stretches from age three to age 21.

By the time they got commissioned at age 21, they had each and all become dead men fighting. By 21, every one of them was already chomping at the bits to take the fight to the Kenimani territory in outer space.

DJ Tate had managed to ingratiate himself with the other veterans enough to become one of the HELL Cadre.

But Justice had kept a close watch on the man, always sniffing out DJ's deep racist leanings without letting on that he suspected anything.

Justice kept in mind his wife's and Sun Tzu's directive: Keep your friends close, and your enemies closer. The Art of War.

Moreover, Justice used Gorgon Brain Nano to keep intimate tabs on DI Tate's festering bigotry.

Justice also had intimate knowledge of DJ's penchant for one of a kind old-school custom-made weapons.

So, over the years, Justice had slowly but surely turned himself into DJ's personal armorer.

And furthermore, he had become some kind of psychologist, almost psychic-expert, regarding how DJ's mind worked to the point where he could predict DJ's next moves, and it would always be as good as money in the bank.

"I started in a hospital. I need to finish it in a hospital. Because except for doctors and nurses, no one ever pays much attention to the sick," Justice said.

"What are you talking about honey?" Timi was getting really concerned. So, she decided to stick with Justice, and let the children and the Robo-servants do irreparable damage to the birthday dishes. For now, she figured her husband needed her way more than the casserole dish did.

"I need to go to the hospital, Timi."

"Why? What's wrong?" The note of alarm in her voice was now palpable.

"Alzheimer's."

"Alzheimer's? Honey, nobody gets Alzheimer's anymore. They eradicated that decades ago," Timi pointed out to her husband.

"Well, Timi, I do! I have just developed an acute case of Alzheimer-like illness. So, I need to be placed in a nursing home right away!"

"BJ, Please, talk to me. What's going on? Why are you talking like this? Is it that simulcast? Maybe you just need to rest up tonight. We'll catch up in the morning."

"Timi, this weekend, please, put me in one of our nursing homes right here in Dam Neck. Please, Timi, just trust me on this one. You make sure none of the doctors or nurses, who work there give me any medicines. You tell them that our concierge doctor is the only one who may prescribe for me, and that you are the only one who can give me the prescribed meds."

"BJ, you're crazy!"

"See? I told you!" Justice retorted.

"No, you know I don't mean it like that. Quit playing!"

"Timi, you're just going to have to trust me on this one, okay?"

"Okay. But for how long are you going to stay there?"

"If my crystal ball serves me correctly, I'd say until the Presidential Inauguration day. So about two and a half months total."

"Jesus! Two and a half months?! BJ, have you lost your mind?!"

"Yes. So, evidently, I do need that nursing home admission real quick. Put me in this weekend. But don't tell anyone that it is temporary. Make everyone -- and I mean everyone, including the kids and the HELL Cadre -- believe it's a permanent arrangement. Please, trust me."

"Alright, BJ. I swear you're going to be the death of me yet. My God, to think I could have fallen for a stable-minded doctor or librarian or teacher or someone normal. But no, not I. I just had to fall in love with the craziest least-stable minded man on the planet! I mean, like who admits themselves into a damn nursing home faking a disease that was wiped out decades ago?!"

"Well, you need to remember that some of us hold-outs refused to take those vaccines, honey."

"BJ, you did take the vaccine. I was there. We both took it together. "

"Not that I can recall...maybe my shot didn't work. You never know!"

"You know what, BJ? I'm done. I'm not going to argue with you about this. So, you wanna go to a nursing home? Fine, I'mma put your behind in a nursing home, and I hope to God the smells in there make you gag!"

"This weekend, Timi" Justice pressed.

"Yes, this doggone weekend, BJ!" Timi stormed away. Their fights were rare, and they always involved Timi storming off, and Justice rooting around in the fridge for a stash of Ben & Jerry's Ice Cream. Once he found the flavor of the week, he would prepare two helpings, one for her, and a pretend-one for himself, which of course, Timi, would end up 'helping' him with. Then, she would melt in his arms way before all the ice cream had melted in her mouth. It never failed.

Today

To go from being the son of a President to being a double-Presidential assassin, DJ thought as he cradled and caressed the double-header rifle he had wangled out of his demented old nemesis, Black 'BJ' Justice, the legendary Commandant of HELL, the hero of Hannibal 2.0 Assault Against the Kenimani.

Rogue1, that's what The Old Man had been called in his hey-day as a Special Operator, DJ continued to reminisce as he awaited the abomination about to happen. Two women, one Black and the other white, were about to swear to become Co-Presidents of his DJ's father's and forefather's country. *Abomination! Over my dead body*, he thought.

And their stupid husbands, each of whom is the brother of the other Co-President-to-be…the husbands would become Vice-Presidents.

Insult upon injury! Not on my damned watch!, DJ thought.

And what a perfect touch that the rifle still bore fingerprints belonging to BJ, the self-proclaimed master armorer!

This is like multidimensional chess, DJ thought, with himself playing the role of the ultimate All-American Grandmaster achieving multiple checkmates with a single move.

This rifle, this double-header of a monster, custom-built for just a purpose such as this, this rifle which BJ, it's maker had proudly called The Iron Fan because it had multiple barrels that could be made to fan out to cover specific targets and tag them all with a single trigger-squeeze, this was the rifle that he, Richard Tate, Jr. would use to mete out justice to the man who deprived him of his glory, his Medal of Honor, and it was the same weapon he would use to course-correct America's head-long crash into the abyss of neo-liberal decadence.

Take out the two Co-Presidents and the two Co-Vice-Presidents. And let the rifle be discovered by the authorities with Black Justice's finger-prints all over it. No nursing home alibi would ever stand. America would demand blood, and the country would pounce on the first available scapegoat. Everyone will be more than eager to crucify Black Justice for this!

DJ Tate made one final scope adjustment. Corrected for windage and temperature one last time. The ceremony that he would end was about to get under way.

DJ blew softly into his raised gloved hands in the manner of a prayer. He rubbed his hands together.

He was ready.

Mrs. Brandee Woolsley-Taylor, hand in hand with her best friend, and soon-to-be Co-President – Mrs. Brenda Taylor-Woolsley walked to the rostrum where the Chief Justice of the United States Supreme Court cheerfully awaited the ladies and their husbands.

Right at the very moment when the Co-Presidents placed their palms on the Holy Bible to swear the Oath of Office, DJ Tate squeezed the trigger of The Iron Fan.

The 7.62's stayed locked in the chambers.

Tasers and stingers shot backwards into DJ Tate's head and neck.

He was instantly paralyzed from head to toe, with the only functions he could control being breathing and blinking. His last thought before he lost control of his cognitive function was, *The Old Man did warn me to watch its six...the old bastard did warn me to watch out for the trick rifle!*

The CRISPR'ed viral vectors immediately went to work.

The transmitter in The Iron Fan sent an alert signal and GPS coordinates to an app on Black Justice's phone-tattoo.

Justice called his wife to secure his discharge from her nursing home.

Timi was ready. She had been ready from Day One! She filled out the paperwork, and got her husband back into the real world.

"Honey, I think you should order us some decent dinner outfits. We are attending some Inaugural Balls tonight!"

"BJ, even by your highly irregular standards, this is all coming across as particularly strange behavior. What's really going on?"

"Cat's in the bag, my queen. I just nailed the last racist on Earth this morning. Or rather, I just helped him to permanently change his ways. Hold on. Let me place a couple of calls to my contacts in the Secret Service.

"They need to go hospitalize an assassin who is now in a locked-in state. I just arrested him, and locked him up inside his own body. From now, until the day he dies he will only be able to blink and breathe."

"BJ, let me get this straight. You're sitting here next to me in this UBER-copter, but you have just arrested a racist-assassin and locked him up inside his own body so that all he can do is blink and breathe?"

"You got it! As soon as you told me Brenda and Brandee won the election, I knew that racist creep, Richard Tate, Jr, would try to assassinate them. I also instinctively knew where, when and how he would try to take out the new Co-Presidents. That man is a creature of habit. So, I had prepped the perfect weapon for him to get the job done during the campaigns, in case those young ladies won the election. And then I had casually told him about The Iron Fan just as a gambit to prep him for a day he might want to 'borrow it' to shoot you and me together.

"That's why when I moved into the nursing home, I told you to call him up to come by and collect all my weapons.

"I deliberately planted The Iron Fan among the hum-drum weapons. I knew he would not be able to resist the idea of using a weapon with my fingerprints on it to carry out his assassination plans.

"I set the trap, and like the son of Richard Tate that he is, he fell headlong into it.

"Thing is I had rigged The Iron Fan to not shoot bullets forward but rather to shoot a taser and tiny auto-syringe-stingers backwards.

"That was the real reason I call it The Iron Fan. It blows backwards.

15

"Anyway, once the Taser immobilizes him, the viral vectors in the stingers would get in his bloodstream very fast.

'In less than five seconds, the CRISPR'ed viruses would have completely peeled away the myelin sheath covering portions of his brain stem. Then boom! I got him! HIs body becomes its own prison.

"From then on, all he will ever be able to do is is remain in his locked-in state, fully aware of everything around him but unable to do anything other than to blink. And to breathe.

"My God, BJ…You are the greatest! But you are also diabolical!"

"No, my Goddess Timi….It is you who are the greatest. And also divine!"

"There you go again, twisting my words all up for your crazy comebacks!" Timi smiled. "I'm sure you know too well what I meant when I said, 'My God!"

Without skipping a bit, Justice said, "As long as you know what I mean when I say 'my Goddess'." He winked at her.

When the Secret Service, the FBI and the Washington DC and Capitol police arrived at the crime scene at the top of the Washington Monument, they found a woman lying stiffly next to a strange weapon. The weapon featured multiple barrels. The whole thing was regarded as a marvel of custom-designed engineering.

The crime scene forensic photographers were flashing away as professionally as they could.

But everyone kept a very wary eye on the 'woman who looked like an alien.'

The woman, as far as the authorities were concerned, had to be some kind of alien, because she was half-black and half-white. Clearly biracial, but in a weird way: the left side of her body was all white, and the right side was all Black.

Stranger still was her eerie resemblance to the two new Co-Presidents of the United States.

On the left side, the suspect looked identical to Mrs, Brenda Taylor-Woolsley, and on the right side, she looked identical to Mrs. Brandee Woolsley-Taylor. All blonde and blue-eyed on one side, and all Afro'ed up with a soulful brown eye on the other side.

The leader of the Secret Service team stepped discreetly away to one side, and placed an encrypted call to an unlisted number.

16

"Hey Rogue, you said there was a tracking device in the assassin's weapon," the Secret Service Agent said, barely above a whisper into his phone-mic-tattoo, "And you also told me I would find DJ Tate and the weapon here at the crime scene."

"And?" Justice asked nonchalantly.

"Well, boss, I found a strange weapon alright, but what I also found here is a freak, a chimeric half-Black, half-white alien creature who looks like the two halves of her were made from halves of our new Co-Presidents! No bloody sign of DJ Tate anywhere around her, BJ. What we've got here is a freaking monster instead of Tate."

"Jack," Justice said, sounding weary, "listen to me carefully. The monster you are looking for, and the monster you just found are one and the same individual. The woman you're looking at is…was DJ Tate. Trust me!" And he disconnected before Jack   could   respond.

The Inaugural Ball at the White House turned out to be one big old contest among sparkling things: chandeliers, diamonds, ice cubes and champagne flutes and bubbles.

People of all colors and races mingled, freely engaging in serious conversations and still managing to laugh easily at one another's jokes.

The Justices had already run into Dr. Randall Robinson and his wife, Mrs. Ariel Robinson -- the nurse he met at John Henrik Clarke Hospital in Igbo Landing, in St Simons Island, Georgia.

Prior to catching up with the Robinsons, the Justices had run into Professor Jimmy Greenlee, the best dressed man at the ball, and his beautiful Afro-Caribbean wife, Mrs. Stella Greenleee.

Justice also recognized the professor from his time at the John Henrik Clarke Hospital, but he wisely did not broach the subject.

As the Justices took a brief pause in their mingling, BJ felt a light tap on his left shoulder. Timi was smiling as he turned around to see who was behind him.

"Well, top of the evening to you," Justice said, bowing slightly, "and on behalf of my wife and myself, I hereby extend to you our heartfelt congratulations on your historic election, Mesdames President."

"Why, thank you," said the two Co-Presidents. "It is great to see you both, Dr. And Mrs. Justice. Thank you for accepting our invitation."

"The honor, privilege and pleasure are most definitely ours," the Justices finished together.

President Woolsley-Taylor and President Taylor-Woolsley both raised their hands in a subtle invitation signal to a white-gloved butler who was standing discreetly off to the side.

The butler, bearing an antique silver-domed cloche, presented himself with great alacrity and pomp next to the Co-Presidents and the Justices.

The Co-Presidents signaled the butler to open the cloche. He did so and simultaneously offered the Justices, "Cookies?"

Justice and Timi reached for a cookie each.

"They are for sale," Co-President Taylor-Woolsley said.

"The cookies are for sale?" Justice asked, his hand frozen midway to delivering the cookie to his mouth. Timi's hand froze on the way to picking her cookie.

"These are no ordinary cookies, Dr. Justice," Co-President Woolsley-Taylor deadpanned. "These are Girl Scout cookies…they happen to be the very best cookies in the whole Laniakea Supercluster!"

Black Justice took a bite, closed his eyes and managed to look totally blissed out as he said, "Hmmm…yummy!"

"Well, we are awaiting your order, Sir," Co-President Taylor-Woolsley prompted.

"Oh, yes, of course, orders," Justice responded. "Please put us down for 25 truckloads of these."

Mrs. Justice's eyes widened, "Did you just say 25 truckloads of Girl Scout cookies, honey?"

"I was thinking, you, me, the children, the grandkids and 25 million of our closest friends and neighbors," Justice responded, reaching for another cookie in the cloche. "You think maybe we should order some more?"

"No, that's just fine, dear. I think 25 truckloads of Laniakea cookies will be quite enough for now. I think we can always reach out to the Presidents for more if we ever run short." Mrs. Justice responded.

"Try one, honey," Justice encouraged his wife. "These are really good cookies. They'll be perfect with your Ben & Jerry's!"

"Dr. Black Justice!" Mrs. Timi Justice exclaimed in mock shock. "Whose team are you really on?"

"TeamGod!" Justice said, smiling.

We've now come to the end of this episode.

But the story of Black Justice has only just begun. Stay tuned!

Very Important To-Do List:

1) Please help us change the world by being fair, just and decent toward everyone you interact with, regardless of their ethnicity, nationality,

religion, gender, creed, fame or lack thereof, fortune or lack thereof, or sexual identity or preferences.

2) Help us spread the word on Social Media, among friends and co-workers about this novel.

3) Give us five stars on Amazon. Please.

4) Form your own local, friends-circle or family-circle or online-circle to discuss this book

5) Create and submit your own better-world quotes and ideas for publication on our website. (Contact us at www.BlackJustice.com for further details. The websites maybe undergoing construction to add this functionality. Please, check back often.)

6) Keep in mind at all times the words of Edmund Burke: "All that is necessary for evil to succeed is for good people to do nothing." So, if you don't do something, the evil people in this world will win.

7) Another fellow said, "Be the change you wish to see in the world!" Be that change. Will you commit to join us today to be the change YOU hope to see in the world.

8) Please remember to recommend us to your family and friends…and even to your haters…maybe especially to the haters!! 😂 😂

9) Remember nobody gave you your life. So, nobody has the right to take it from you. (Google Fela's lyrics: "Uniform na cloth; na tailor de sew am!") Fear not!

10) Always be ready to do whatever it takes to defend yourself, and to defend the just.

Discussion Ideas

A. Do you believe [the world] is perfect right now?

B. If you believe [the world] is not perfect, what can you do personally to make it better?

C. If you have figured out what you can do, are you already doing it! If not, why not? Who or what is holding you back?

Alright, now let's do this:

You see how the words "the world" is bracketed in the first two questions above? Now please go ahead and at your pace, substitute the following words for the bracketed words.

1. Your life
2. Your family
3. Your workplace
4. Your school
5. Your marriage
6. Your city
7. Your state
8. Your country
9. Your health

10. Your religious beliefs and practices
11. Your knowledge and understanding
12. Your charitable activities

For more community discussion, join us on BlackJustice.com to talk about any of the above topics and let us know if we can help you to make the world a better place.

Acknowledgments

I owe a debt of gratitude to many who helped to incubate all the elements needed to produce this work:

Micia. Thank you for giving me the time and space I needed to focus on writing.
Tshaun, Jamila, Kim, Tasha, Quetta, Julene, Joyce, Tarah, Megan, Theresa, Yemisi. Thank you for the support.
Seminole. Thank you for typing the first draft.
Jibola Bakare, Bike Bakare and Motunde Dosunmu. Thank you for helping to gather some acknowledgment information.
Serena Gay and Shaddai Frazier (My God-children…I never forgot you. More on that later.) Thank you for your patience.

My belated gratitude to my ancestors for their forbearance with my slow pace of awakening:
Alhaji Salu Onirakunmi, Alhaji and Alhaja Animashaun, Alhaja Khadijah Kubrah Agbalaiya, Alhaja Sherifat Adebisi Bakare, Mrs. Silifat Adenike Ige-Adubi Laguda, Baba Oni Lentriki Agbalaiya, Iya Eleran Agbalaiya (Nee Aro-Lambo), Mr. Yekeen Agbalaiya, Mr. F. O. Bakare, Chief N. A. O. Dosunmu, Madam Adiat Bashorun, Hon. Justice Latif Jinadu Dosunmu, Mr. Raufu Ajadi Dosunmu, Mr. Waheed Jinadu Dosunmu, Alhaji Ganiyu Kolawole Dosunmu, Alhaji Jinadu Sunmola Olaonipekun Dosunmu, Alhaja Ajarat Olaide Dosunmu (Nee Danmole), Alhaji Salmon Danmole, Madam Abusatu Ayoka Dosunmu (Mama Sapele), Chief Sunmola Fasanya Dosunmu, Chief Majalu Dosunmu, Madam Orejokale Onikoyi, Madam Idewu Oshobile Eletu-Odibo, Chief Oshobile Eletu Odibo, Alhaja Ganiat Ejide Dosunmu, Madam Sikirat Adunni Dosunmu, Alhaja Raliat Adeboye, Mr. Muniru Olaseni Dosunmu. I bow my head down low to the ground for all of you. Gbogbo yin pata pata ni moki oo, lalai f'enikan. Ki e sun re oo. O wa d'arinnoko, otun wa d'oju ala oo!

Majalu Dosunmu:
Omo ogbiya ni sasi; Omo omi nla ti se opa kere; Omo akenigbo k'eru o ba ara ona; Omo ogbiya afigbe gboran;
Omo adogan feyinti o n'wo se dana;
O n'wo awon asebi, bi won ti se 'nse ara won;
Omo a ke fun d'agba l'ode Ibeshe;
Omo o wu bantun; Omo magbin-magbin dundun
Omo aden, omo alaragbo, a sun b'oye ji
Omo onijegi opa-arooo
Omo olowo j'oye meji po, t'ogbe iketa hanu;
Omo erin o beji, omo erin beji o ya so;
Omo onile a te jeje, ajoji a te girigiri;
Omo a kan luda ma f'ara kan omi
Ibini a rokun tayoooo

Fasanya Sunmola Dosunmu:
Adara loye oko Adubi; Eni to so wipe osu yi kole to, ki owun na gun akaba.

Jinadu Sunmola Dosunmu:
Olaonipekun, Omo ogbiya ni sasi;
Omo ake fun d'agba l'ode Ibeshe;
Omo akenigbo k'eru o ba ara ona;
Omo omi nla ti se opa kere;
Omo alaragbo, a sun b'oye ji; Omo onijegi oparo.

Alhaja Eleha Olaide Danmole:
Omo oni Saro awonga; Omo onibu eja kiki abasha;
Saro n'gbagba ni yawo, ot'arugbo she l'oge
Omo oni Saro aromimawe.

Eletu Odibo:
Iba e o Osobile baba Idewu. Idewu to bi Dosunmu si Idunmagbo, je ko ye wa loni
oo!

Agbalaiya:
Omo a je Idofian le'nmefa lemo lemo!

And I also owe an eternal debt of gratitude to my head-instructors:
Mr. Abaniwonda, Mr. Bakare, Mr. Bello, Mama (Ansar-Ud-Deen School)
Mr. Olasiji Layeni, Mr. Otutuloro, Mama Gbadamosi (Ansar Ud-Deen Grammar School)
Mr. J.O. Olatunbosun; Mr. Beckley; Tigress (Igbobi College)
Dr. Dosekun, Dr. and Dr. (Mrs.) Elebute, Dr. Femi-Pearse, Dr. Akinla, Dr. Ashiru, Dr. Lasi, Dr. Okuwobi, Dr. Araba, Dr. Lesi, Dr. Ransome-Kuti, Dr. Esho, Dr. Mabadeje (College of Medicine, University of Lagos.)
Dr. Alfred, Dr. Mattox, Dr. Gaston, Dr. Smith, Dr. Oxley, Dr. Bharmal, Judge Celeste, Ms. Burns, Dr. Herbert, Dr. Garrison (Morehouse School of Medicine)
Dr. Kohane (CHIP)
I understand that no amount of acknowledgment can ever make up for all the years of headaches I caused most of you. I apologize. They say the arrow that must fly far, must first be nocked and drawn way back. Nice saying; terrible excuse, I know. But it's the best I can do for now. Sorry. Love you all.

No justice, no peace.

Black Justice Forever!

Soli Deo Gloria!

www.ingramcontent.com/pod-product-compliance
Lightning Source LLC
Chambersburg PA
CBHW060258150626
46556CB00022B/2744